THE MO]

THE MONKEY STATE

J. R. ROBERTS

TOUCAN TALES

Book Cover by Mark Horton
Map by Melissa Nash
Edited & Typeset by Anamchara Editing

ISBN 978-1-0683228-0-8 (paperback)
ISBN 978-1-0683228-1-5 (ebook)

TOUCAN TALES

To the escape artists, idealists and thinkers …
It's okay to play, it's okay to dream and sometimes, it's okay to just be.

In loving memory of Nans.
She passed away on Boxing Day 2024 after an incredible innings of one hundred and two years.
Wishing you the best in the world beyond the mist.

Prologue

Flight Of The Toucan

There is only one law under the canopy: trust your own judgement.

- Reginald Saei -

The Toucan took off from his treetop perch, out on the other side of things, where the rain did not fall as hard or for as long. The sun shone brighter, the colours more vivid. Soaring, weaving, this way and that, he embraced the rush of air to his face. A glimpse of deep blue sky against a deeper sea of green. Savouring his last few moments high above the canopy, he began to descend, slipping through the rooftop, darting between trees, swooping through gaps. Easing his flight offered an opportunity to appreciate its true beauty. Some called it Maya, others paradise. To him, it was simply calm.

Slowly, though, things started to turn gloomy. The landscape stretched out across a great ravine of jungle. He soon came to the shore of a raging murky river, the current frothing dangerously far below. Its warning sounds reached even his ears. He eyed the

1

abyss warily as he crossed into darker climbs. The air became sticky, filled with the thrum of heavy industry, trees being viciously felled, giant structures being built, hordes of monkeys hard at work. Greys and browns had taken over from the vibrant colours. Most of the other animals had long since fled, and who could blame them?

"Left brain, left brain," he jabbered to the air, "it's all they use." He peered down at an active group of individuals, their eyes firmly forward. *These monkeys are not so arboreal,* he thought, feathers ruffling. Swooping a little closer to their pod-like homes, he wondered why they chose to live so close to the ground. So much more freedom in the air. Freedom to move. Never contained. The chance to follow the wind, not that there was even a whisper of it round here.

Unable to linger, he continued on, pained by what he saw. A picture of destruction, oppression and grind. He kept himself far enough out of sight, pitching and rolling among some canopy climbers.

Eventually the Toucan found what he was looking for. A solitary figure. The familiar hunched shoulders, a furrowed brow. Living life without really living. The monkey, tall and strong of frame, dragged his tail absentmindedly along the rainforest floor. As the bird found a spot to simply observe, he caught the tiniest glimpse of vibrant green. A spark of life amid the gloom. The monkey came to a halt, a puzzled look forming across his features, eyes turning upwards and scanning the canopy.

Does he sense I'm here?

He took a careful hop back on the branch and shuffled his feathers discreetly. *No*, he did not believe he had been spotted. Yet, it took time before the monkey was at peace again—if that is what it could be called. The Toucan asked the neighbouring trees, "Ready, I wonder?"

The trees did not respond, of course, and the monkey continued about his business, lolloping back towards his civilisation. He shot one last lingering glance at the canopy before the hunched shoulders returned and he disappeared from view.

Surely the monkey had not been close enough to see the colours of the Toucan's eye and beak; that was a piece of fortune. It was not the way of things for a bird to show itself before a monkey was truly ready.

When he was sure no one else was around, the bird hovered for a few moments in contemplation, then arced out in a graceful circle, allowing a view of their entire world. Taking a different route, eastward, away from the oppressive heat and stifling atmosphere, he headed over the imposing monkey-made wall that locked the Tribe within their borders.

Once he escaped, the relief was immense. Blue skies greeted his eyes, along with cooler airspace. He was soaring now, enjoying the flight. Swooping left, barrelling right, dropping down, then shooting up, the flight of the Toucan was a rare sight to behold. The colours had returned now, and vast pools of fresh water glinted back reflections of the warm sun. Luvé—life's quiet pulse—remained untainted here. Animals were playing, thriving once more. He could make out his familiar treetop palace. Other birds were about the place, chattering away.

"You okay, Alvis?" asked a pretty female.

He nodded politely and hopped past her. He did not have time for idle flirtation right now, only for thought. The short reconnaissance mission had been accomplished, worth the trip, for sure. Alvis settled into his nest, tucked into one of the giant banyan trees that graced the wider rainforest, and welcomed the delightful spray of the water teasing him. It cooled his heart, and he exhaled deeply. *Is it time?*

Chapter One

New Moon, Same Story

The desire to escape is the natural response to extrinsic compulsion.
If untamed, it may haunt your days. Your nights. And your dreams.

- J. Semmelwise Locke -

He lay motionless in the darkness of his pod. Eyes open, gaze fixed on the shifting shadows, unable to return to sleep. The rain had stopped its relentless barrage. Replaced by the incessant drips of water from the canopy outside. Uneasiness filled his bones. Restlessness laced his mind. A longing to escape his suffocating confines. It was not a normal desire—no monkey had ever left Tierra Libre—so the history books told anyway.

The menacing cry of the howlers echoed through the rainforest. Claude Talador cursed, rolling onto the other side of his bunk. He reached to the bedside table and shoved his earplugs in. But the calls were too ferocious, rumbling like a storm. They could not be blocked out; that was the point of the morning alarm after all.

He hauled himself up and climbed down to the communal kitchen. There he lit a small fire, beginning his morning ritual, heating the water and brewing his beans. The smell of fresh roasted coffee aroused the interest of his fellow pichu monkeys, most of whom, with vacant eyes, demanded a cup. Once he had served the ungrateful regulars, he worked on a final one. For himself. He carried it in his tail, back to the comfort of his drab little dwelling, among so many others in Dormor 43.

More howls rattled the timber frame of his room; the entire structure creaked and buckled. A crack he had not bothered to address allowed a beam of dawn-time light to fill the place. He picked absentmindedly at a few fresh bites and sipped in silence.

The dream had been clear enough. A feathered creature perched way up high. Its inquisitive black eye, encased in a blue lid, blinking. Tracking his movements. Not for the first time. He wondered why it never spoke, only watched.

He scrubbed his teeth, hoping to mask the dark stains, and dragged a comb through his thick fur—the small patches of green the only real signs of life. It did not take long for him to give up on the stubborn knots. No need for excessive grooming.

"Another day in paradise," Claude whispered, hauling his satchel over his shoulder and slamming the door shut.

His neighbours had already left, not that they talked much. He moved into the damp rainforest of muted greens and dull browns. A persistent drizzle did nothing to mask an already oppressive heat. His four limbs took him without much thought, and he certainly did not rush as he passed under the vast timber sign with the words etched: *No Monkey Business.*

***

Many would be excited today, Claude was not. A vast group sat with heads bowed before a raised stage. Slipping in towards the back, he moved quietly, the hushed atmosphere punctuated only by the sound of heavy breathing. Quickly, he dropped into meditation. He closed his eyes, pretending to visualise gratitude for the State, the Monvida and his *wonderful* family. As he wrestled to maintain the facade, a sharp whistle pierced the air, signalling the end of this practice.

He opened his eyes to the sight of their leader sat on a grand wooden throne at the centre of the stage—a truly giant monkey adorned with official regalia, including a headdress of woven leaves. Her golden eyes surveyed the audience. A quartet of hormiga monkeys entered, carrying instruments. The State servants set about beating the drums, creating a low throbbing sound. Steady and light to begin with, the beat soon increased in volume. She raised her arm; the drums stopped. Her lip curled in a possible smile.

"Welcome, welcome, my pichus," she said. "Welcome to the new Green Moon in Tierra Libre. A time of significant progress lies ahead. I trust it will be prosperous for you all. The State is at your service." She bowed low.

Well, as far as her immense frame would allow.

"We believe in the Holy One," murmured the crowd.

"Our Monvida."

A fuller smile spread across her features.

Always so unnatural, thought Claude.

"There has not been a better time to be a member of this Tribe," she said. "Water and food are in excellent supply. I do not know of one pod-less monkey in our trees. We have invested heavily in facilities, tools for industry and improvements to the Easthaven Wall. There have been reports of new disturbances in Shadowbor, so we must be ever vigilant."

Claude snarled at the mention of that place, too far back for anyone to notice. But, it was still dangerous to show any sign of dissent. Especially in front of the hormigas.

The Monvida continued. "Please trust that we will keep you safe. Safe from the dangers we all know lurk beyond our canopy—"

No one really knew. Although, the Taladors knew a little more than most.

"Anyway"—she cleared her throat—"despite these positives, the work does not stop. We must keep our Eyes Forward. Growth is good for everyone. Continued upgrades to our lifestyles require ever more high-quality timber. We are simply not producing enough. I will need your full efforts in the moons to come. To find the answers. The solutions."

Everyone knew of the growing timber shortage in the Tribe. Quite how desperate it was, most dared not ask.

"As a sign of my gratitude," she said, "salaries for all State officials will be increased by at least two percent."

The proclamation brought whispers of delight from most of the audience.

Claude rolled his eyes. *But at what cost, Your Holiness?*

"But," she announced, "this does mean a tiny change. Formal work hours will be increased, ever so slightly. The final whistle will now sound at 8 p.m. I trust this will not cause any inconvenience to most of you; it is not like you must finish on the dot anyway."

"Exactly," said Dubbert Grouse, Claude's scrawny neighbour and colleague. "Too much Monkey Business these days if you ask me."

"I don't see it somehow," said Claude, calculating the working week would now be a delightful eighty-four hours of forced servitude.

The Monvida drawled on. "As always, if you have any questions, any ideas for how to improve things or if you notice anything suspicious with a fellow pichu—curfew breaches, for example—do be so kind as to mention it to a hormiga or Acolyte. In confidence, of course."

Claude almost choked at the thought of *in confidence* in Tierra Libre. And anything could be twisted to fit the needs of the State. Dubbert shot him a look of disgust, pointing back at the stage.

"Speaking of my Acolytes," she said, "please come on up."

A small group of pompous-looking monkeys came to rest next to their leader. None of them were close to the bulk of the Monvida, or at least that was the way it was staged. They formed a tight semi-circle behind her, grinning out at those below.

She touched each on the shoulder. "Together, we will continue to address the more critical matters of life. These monkeys work faster, and harder, than one could dare to imagine. Please be upstanding and thank them for their continuing contributions."

The sound of applause rang out, but Claude remained still, focused on the movement at the side of the crowd. A number of hormigas moved in. Some held long whips. Some brandished pointed spears. Some even wielded wooden swords, sharp enough to cause serious damage.

"Thank you, thank you," said the Monvida as the noise died down. "Well, look how time has flown. Please make your way to the start of the Commute. This will now be five full laps, starting today."

The latest announcement brought genuine grumbles.

"Hush, hush," she replied, clearly expecting the response. "It is so we are better prepared for the challenges ahead. Most of you monkeys are sat down all day anyway."

"She's not wrong." Dubbert chuckled.

"May the fire of Fuerza be in your hearts." The Monvida concluded with another awkward bow, and a chant swept through the crowd. *Pichu, Pichu, Pichu!*

As the voices rose, Claude kept his focus on one particular Acolyte. So smarmy, so serious and now so overweight. The position had not been kind to her. He grinned as she struggled, along with the others, to raise their leader off the stage.

His enjoyment was short-lived. A sharp jab to the ribs. One of the more vicious-looking hormigas pulled back its blade, scowled and indicated towards the exit. Claude bristled, puffing up his chest, readying his tail. He reared up. At least twice its size. *I could end you. In a heartbeat.*

And yet, a glint of sunlight flickered against the varnish of the State servant's sword. And with it, the thought of rebellion vanished.

Chapter Two

Monkeys In Cubicles

Work has become the defining verb of our culture. Monkeys that used to play in the trees now work in the cubicles engineered from the tree's timber. Work earns them a living. Work gives them purpose. Work gives them something to think about. But how much of the work is actually needed? For the Tribe to thrive. Now that is a debate I am keen to expound upon.

—From "The Ordinary Pichu – A History of Work"
by Aldous Musk.

Unlike many of the other pichus, Claude's breath came in steady, measured puffs as he completed his laps of the Commute at a decent pace. Such speed always worth it, buying a few seconds before the day of drudgery ahead. Taking cover under a gnarled grey palm, its fronds doing little to shield him from the rain, he swung his satchel round and rummaged through the damp contents.

He pulled out a bosky—*dry enough*—and tucked it between his teeth as he pulled out a tiny glowing orb of luvé, its subtle warmth pulsing in his palm. He cupped it close to the bosky's tip, shielding it from the rain as the amber glow flared, coaxing a brief spark that smouldered his smoke to life.

The first drag met his lungs with the same undeniably foul taste he had come to expect, one he forced down anyway. A strange form of relief.

A round-faced pichu with growing bald patches approached, sweat dripping from his brow and pretty much everywhere else. "Wait for me, young chap, will you?" he said between gasps.

"Only if you speed up a little, old chap."

The monkey wiped his brow. "Us older townies aren't appreciated in our time."

Claude slouched against the trunk of the palm. "You're not even old."

"Well, you try working on Floor 9 for over two hundred moons," said Karo, skin flaking as he scratched the spots on his crown. "Always more demands. Always more inspections. And the paperwork—it never used to be this bad. I can see where all the bloody bark goes. And now five laps. It's not sustainable for pichus like me. I can feel the pain in my heart. Bo will be furious; she'll be wanting her fur groomed till dawn. Plus, it's raining. Again!"

"It's always raining here"—Claude deftly put his arm around Karo—"now is just not the time to moan about it."

A couple of hormigas at a distance fixed their eyes on them. One held a long whip that could no doubt reach them if desired.

Karo nodded with a huff and curse up towards the thickening gloom before his gaze dropped to the muddy ground.

Claude led his colleague onwards, the journey slow. Something he had come to expect whenever Karo was involved. He had to chuckle—pichus were not genetically wired for speed across the ground—a fact painfully evident by Karo's awkward shuffle.

The air grew muggy as they trudged past the thicker trees that formed the entrance to Hussleton. High above, a hormiga sat in one of the giant carved statues that stood guard over the zone. Claude shot it a wink.

A throng of pichus milled to the side of the main office buildings. It was always the same: heads down, voices low, everyone too tired to notice just how small their world had become. A perfect reflection of the State's grip—productive, orderly.

"You go on ahead," Karo mumbled. "Said I'd help this lot with the new five-day-workweek petition."

Claude took one last puff and chucked his bosky to the wet turf. "Good luck with that," he said, joining the queue of grumpy caffeinated monkeys at the entrance.

As he passed through the turnstiles, a familiar sinking feeling flowed through his fur. He waved his badge and ambled towards the base of the lift, waiting patiently for it to fill. It cranked up, the heat rising with each elevation. The poster of revered worker Monkei Starkov stared back at him. Her crimson fur, bushy brows and smug narrowing of the eyes suggested you dare try to compete with me. Claude scoffed. Fraud. No one worked one hundred-hour weeks. Not even the so-called State heroes. His gaze shifted to the others in the lift. A collection of truly worried souls. Their nervous tics and self-absorption suggested they were not used to cutting it this fine for the start of the working day.

The opening whistle blew just before the lift reached Floor 9. Claude yawned and sauntered into the office without a shred of urgency. Why rush? He had long since mastered the art of time-dumping—creating an elaborate fiction of all the work he would supposedly complete on a given day. If Fuerza were watching, even the God of Work himself might have applauded his mastery of the illusion.

"What time do you call this?" said a pichu with large walnut-coloured eyes, glancing up from her work.

Claude dived into his cubicle chair, spinning round a couple of times. "You heard the whistle, Maitri."

"We have start times for a reason, you know. It's not fair if it's one rule for one, one rule for another. It'll soon cause chaos." She tutted.

"Chaos," said Claude, "what a terrible thought."

She poked her head over the top of the divide, ears pricked. "You been up to mischief again?"

If anyone else had asked that, he would have snapped. But Beena Maitri was different. A good monkey, all things considered. "Far from it," he said. "But someone had to keep an eye on our esteemed colleague."

The bumbling Karo entered, fur askew. He hurried towards his private office, tossing a quick nod at the two of them, a relieved grin on his face. A grin promptly wiped off when a hormiga bobbed purposefully in his direction.

Claude raised an eyebrow and spun his chair to face the scene. Beena followed, chin propped on her hand. The hormiga gesticulated; Karo's tail limper with each muffled word exchanged. Whatever was said was not pleasant. Their colleague slumped from head to tail before he trudged into his office, shutting the door without looking back.

Beena spun back round. "Great job you're doing of that."

"He's simply not that well suited to this line of work."

"Yes"—she smirked, shuffling her papers—"and I wonder how well suited you are for this work, Mr Talador?"

"It's what I've always wanted. What I've always dreamt of."

Claude settled into his workstation, the cramped space pinching in around him. It was more like folding into the desk than sitting, his shoulders brushing both sides of the cubicle. He shifted his weight, trying to get comfortable in a seat that never seemed to fit. With a sigh, he reached for his earplugs and popped them in. The hum of the office dulled, replaced by blessed silence— just the way he liked it. Endless chatter and idle gossip were not welcome in his head. He deplored the office politics that plagued the place.

Pulling out his latest report on *Monkey Output Maximisation*, he found the top corner of the page folded a solid four hundred pages in. Time for his favourite kind of work. No, not the report.

Daydreaming. Specifically, *How in the name of Tiarra did I end up here?*

It was fair to say he had fallen into the role of State Inspector—SIs as they were more commonly known. He had declined all manner of bullshit jobs: coffee bean counter, creative legislator, deep tree rummager, reality enforcement officer, shadow sentry, etc. He had never fancied being a treeper—that would mean spending every single moon turn with Cama, his father. Thankfully he had not been accepted onto the Acolyte Ascension Programme—a vapid bug of an interviewer had made quite sure of that. She had harped on about his above-average potential for Monkey Business. To be fair, she had shown more insight into his character than any of the nosey career development advisers.

Despite all this, the life of an SI was considered prestigious. The pay in aethersalt decent, the prospects likewise. The reality was that the work was bone dry, the hours long, and most of his working life consisted of throwing paper balls into the bin of a stuffy office where the rickety fans broke as often as Dubbert Grouse frowned. An environment shared with mostly boring monkeys, devoid of any real ambition, sat growing fatter as they crept towards the (apparently) juicy mango of retirement.

Welcome to Tierra Libre, a rainforest where fun and freedom are even less abundant than song and sunlight. Claude ticked off the hours, one by one, until the 7 p.m. whistle. *Make that 8 p.m. now!* He carried out this ritual each day, charting the moons on a paper calendar, not entirely sure why. Always with some variation of the thought, *Is this it?*

Chapter Three

Beyond The Mist

*Most monkeys assume the world stops at the edge of
their canopy. That nothing exists beyond their trees.
The occasional monkey climbs right past them.*

—From "The Lost Diaries of Tiarra"

Claude turned down the offer of a night of dice with Karo.
Turned down a trip beneath the trees with his latest female
admirer. Turned down the offer of a three-course dinner with
Beena and her lovely, exceedingly dull family. He wanted to be
alone. A much frowned upon desire in this world, if truth be told.

Leaving Floor 9, he took the lift and passed out of the
turnstiles. A familiar rising feeling in his heart greeted his exit
into the muggy evening rainforest; it had clearly been chucking
it down. Nothing new there. Setting out north, he made his way
through the thicker jungle, away from Hussleton. He thought of
little, keeping his ears open, his movements as silent as possible.
The constant rain created a wall of sound, pattering through the

leaves and branches, masking his presence. Being caught away from a central zone close to curfew was not worth the hassle. A potential flogging never a pleasant prospect. Although neither were the muddies, the pesky flying insects that nipped at his peace at every opportunity. Especially where he was headed.

He soon reached the very edge of Tierra Libre. In the east, a massive timber wall loomed, but here, the territory had a more natural border. Brown, vast and impenetrable. The Agumon River. The great beast frothed and fizzed its way past. Claude went as close as he dared; even the risk of a passing hit by the spray was too grave to take. It could sizzle the fur in an instant.

Ruffling in his satchel, he found his prize, the finely ground leaves, pipe and a drop of luvé. A quick glance around for unwanted visitors—though he did not expect to be troubled—and he readied the concoction. Punk, he knew, was technically illegal. Its psychoactive properties were not the problem as it came from a wattsplant, harmless as any. It was more a question of control; the State did not like their pichus getting dependent. Dependent on anything *they* could not control. The leaf had its own market, which Claude knew well. *Too well.*

Taking a large inhale, he returned his gaze to the muddy tyrant before him. The strong torrents of foam a force of nature, locking all monkeys inside. Their souls too. His eyes were less for the Agumon and more for the thick layer of mist that coated the northern bank, offering an ominous warning from the rainforest that it was not to be crossed. He had always dreamt of adventure.

Always dreamt of escape.

They say I keep dreaming. But it's better than what they do.

Yet it was hard to feel any hope for such things out here. It would take one mighty leap. *Fear's a fiction of the mind;* his mother Sura's voice filled his head. Even though she—

"I wouldn't stand so close, laddie!"

Claude jumped. An ancient pichu with a long stick in her tail edged towards him.

"Dark things come to those that stray near them waters, you know," she muttered, coming to a halt.

"Wonder what's out there though," said Claude, more to himself. "Beyond the mist …"

"Darkness … beyond your wildest imagination. That's what exists out there. My grandfather died in that there poison. I'd say you better take a pichulength back. Or two."

"I see," said Claude, ignoring the offer. *I'll do as I please, you old fossil.*

"Unless you want to die, that is?" She shrugged. "Some do these moons. My time is near anyway. Maybe I should dive in and be done with it. Although I've forgotten how to jump, all that time inside."

"You've come from the Retirement Village?"

She laughed. "Aye, if that's what they call it these days. Ghastly place really. Ghastly! I shouldn't be out here, you know, but everyone needs a little escape sometimes. Ain't that right?" She nudged him with her stick and let out a croaked cackle.

"You're not wrong," he said. "I'd leave tomorrow if I could."

"Leave Tierra Libre? Oh, no, no, no, what a load of Monkey Business. Never been done. Been tried once in a blue moon, maybe. Yet no monkey survived to tell the tale. It's too dangerous out there."

"But you said everyone needs an escape?"

She shook her head. "Oh, no, only if you can come back. Just a wee moment to explore, let your tail hang loose a bit. Not me, laddie. Always happy to return. Back to the comforts of the Tribe. If you were to end up out there"—she waved her stick towards the water—"there'd be no coming back, and we wouldn't want you back neither!"

"Can't say I agree," said Claude, the punk kicking in; he had no time for pandering. "In my dreams I've been beyond it. Seen a wider world full of life and colour. If I could find a way, I'd fly right over."

"Careful what you wish for." She narrowed her eyes. "You may get it."

A flash of colour appeared in the distance above the river. *What the?* The small shape travelled at speed. Through the mist, rising beyond the treeline. Claude rushed closer to the riverbank. Black feathers, wings and a glinting eye. Like the one from his dreams. It swooped over the water. Spun high above the two monkeys. Only there for the briefest of moments. Disappearing. Absorbed back into the cloak of mist above the Agumon, whose water seemed to flow more viciously than ever before. Claude searched for a way across the river. A way to follow it. Leave his prison right now.

Reality hit him with full force. The fear gripped him too. He retreated from the bank, turning his back to it. His legs shook a little as he shifted his weight. The old female hunched over her stick, seemingly studying his pieces of green. "What in the whole of Tierra Libre has come over you?"

"What in the whole of Tierra Libre was that?" Claude pointed to the horizon. "That winged thing."

"Yer talking gibberish."

He rubbed his eyes. "You didn't see it then?"

"See what?" she said. "I'm quite an old lassie if you hadn't noticed. Don't see much at all now."

"It was a bird," Claude said, his tone sharpening. "I'm sure of it."

She snorted. "Birds! They've not been seen in these parts since the great fire of the Red Claw Moon. You need to lay off the wattsplant a little. Makes you go funny if you're not careful. Get yourself back to your pod if I were you. You don't know how good you got it; move as free as you want after work." She turned back south. "I better get back too before they set the howlers on me. Not that I'd mind, I guess. Would end things nice and quick. None of this *waiting* around."

With a final wave of her stick, she departed, muttering as she went. "Birds? He's having you on, dear. No chance."

***

Claude let her go, knowing full well what he had seen. He cracked out the last of his punk, savouring the kick. But it did not help. Not really. The unease rolled in anyway, a barrelling current he could not fight off. It hit him hard, stark, unsettling.

Loneliness. That is what it was. That not one single pichu seemed to share his intrigue for the unknown, his desire to explore, to even consider there *could* be a world beyond the mist.

The cry of a howler struck his ears. Even after all these years, a chill passed through him. His fur bristled, right around the nape of his neck. Strange, given the humidity. He shook himself and scanned the forest floor, scrabbling around. Searching for something—anything sharp enough. His hand closed around a gnarly yucca, edge pointed. He pricked his right index finger. A bead of blood grew. Coaxing a few drops, he flicked his hand, speckling the drips around his shoulders. Another howl pierced the muggy air. Closer this time. Much closer.

"So it begins," he whispered to the trees.

He gripped the rough bark of the nearest palm, his first pull nearly slipped. His hands and feet scrambled for purchase against the trunk. A sharp pain tore through his forearms—muscles unused to such demands—but he gritted his teeth, hauled himself upwards.

At the first sturdy branch, his arms trembled, chest heaved. He looked down—the ground below impossibly distant. Then up—the canopy a maze of twisting limbs and shadows.

The raging snarls of the howlers replaced the raging sounds of the river and the whizzing of the native vampire bats attracted by the scent of blood added to the thrill.

Can I do this?

His first leap was blind—a desperate lunge into the void. He flailed for the next branch, fingers barely latching on as his body swung wildly, legs kicking for balance. The next jump came no easier—too far, he might tumble; too close, and he risked losing momentum. His tail, clumsy at first, found its purpose—a crucial fifth limb. No time to celebrate. There was a hunter not that far from that tail.

Glancing back, its hulking frame came into view. Thrashing jaws, the messy spew of bile, blazing red eyes. *Why would they breed such a thing?*

Claude dropped to the canopy floor, allowing the beast to catch a good whiff of his scent. It was on the ground too, pounding through the undergrowth. Its snarling breaths growing louder, closing in.

A few seconds away now.

He crouched, facing his foe. The howler opened its mouth wide. The stench of its breath. Disgusting. Ready to—

Claude sprang up. Over its head. The creature's jaw snapped beneath him, narrowly missing his tail. The next roar was positively unholy. He did not look back, scaling another large trunk. He switched his climb speed to fast. As blooming well fast as he could manage. The risk was real, muscles straining. A missed branch, a failed jump, would leave him as supper for these vicious animals, and no one would realise that was how he had gone.

He could not stop. Not now.

Being an athletic monkey by pichu standards, a crafty one too, he put distance between himself and the howler. Swooping this way and that. Ignoring the sounds of his pursuer. Focus only on the moment. He was almost back to the main camp; he had almost won. He stopped, finally breathing freely. Considered doubling back for one last date with destiny. Bait them one last time. But other sounds filled the air now. Voices. *Hormigas*. Claude dared not make a sound. He could hear them sniffing.

"There's no one about," one hormiga said. "No Monkey Business here."

"Stupid beasts," said another. "Shame their brains are nowhere near the size of their balls."

Claude forced himself to stay still. *The really stupid species is you.*

Their arrival meant the game was up. For tonight, anyway. He had to reach Dormor 43 before they spotted his green. They would soon control the perimeter.

He slunk his way through the trees, staying low to the ground, the rain coming down hard now. Tricky to see much beyond his nose.

By the time he got back it was well past curfew, and a firm darkness had descended to grip the trees. His neighbours were already cooped up inside, not a single soul about the place, only the crackle of insects. As he climbed up to his pod, the eyes of Dubbert Grouse flashed out from behind the curtain vines of his ground-floor abode. *They say that sham of a pichu peeps on all the comings and goings of our tree!* Claude looked back again—

nothing—the curtain closed. Shaking his head, he dismissed it as the lingering effects of the wattsplant. The Green Moon, now dazzling, cast a spotlight as he shut his door.

He went straight to his bedside table, sliding the drawer open to stow the remaining punk. He wrapped it in taro leaves, then opened *Fuerza's Twelve Rules of Work Efficiency*. Never read. Inside the book, he had carved out a deep circle within the pages. A perfect hiding place. With his stash secured, he washed off the mental fatigue of the workday and clambered into bed.

It took a long while for sleep to arrive. His thoughts seemed to accelerate at just the wrong time. Picking up speed when he needed them to do the opposite. The rough wooden walls of his pod closed in, like when Cama used to grip him by the throat for misbehaving.

It was a treat when the battle ended.

He was flying across the Agumon, dreaming of a new world from an old story. A world not restricted by boundaries. No howlers. No hormigas. No Monvida. In fact, no State at all.

माया

Chapter Four

Imagine, A Bar In The Trees

They say I am a rebel, a troublemaker. But I say I am a champion of the oppressed, a defender of the weak. I will not bow to tyranny nor cower before injustice. I will fight for what is right, even if it means facing the fire of Fuerza itself.

- Kong Wu -

A whole moon phase passed with no other strange occurrences. No more encounters with old demented villagers. No more sightings of birds. No more dreams of flying. Much to Claude's disappointment. Life returned to its mundane best, like the views of Tierra Libre.

As they left Hussleton, Karo grabbed his colleague by the arm. "Know what night it is, chap?"

Claude shrugged, wondering if he could fit in another session at the jungle gym.

"Look," said Karo, pointing towards the sky. The moon was visible on the horizon; it possessed a strange effervescent glow, nothing more.

"It's a full moon," said Claude. "Never seen one of those?"

"Not just any moon, chap, the Blood Red Moon. Marking the night Fuerza consolidated power. Defeating that upstart Cherosa and his group of zealots. A sword was put through all of them and order was established again."

"What a thing to celebrate."

Karo frowned. "We could let our tails down a little?"

"No," said Claude. "You know what'll happen."

"Come on, I need a break from Bo occasionally. Who else can help me?"

Claude could not argue with that. "Where then?"

"The Cashew."

The resident casino. Where I always win a dash of aethersalt, while Karo loses most of his. "Nah, too many townies."

"To the Forager?"

A fast-food eatery, where I might see my lovely sister. "Hell no."

"You wanna go the Drunken Monkey, don't you?"

Bingo! "It's the only place I can relax." Claude shrugged. "Only old treepers to worry about. And they keep themselves to themselves." *Most of them, anyway.*

"Makes me nervous that far out."

"When are you not nervous, my friend?"

"Fine." Karo rolled his eyes. "As long as you get the first round."

As they journeyed south, thick drizzle coated the air. Heading out into those trees was not banned, not even frowned upon, but a pair of townies wanting to go there, where the lower end

28

of pichu society hung out—that was strange. The pair ambled through the Tierra Libre dusk, the canopy hiding any presence of the fabled moon and accentuating the first sounds of the howlers stirring.

"I wonder," Claude said, a smirk playing on his lips, "what we did before the howlers?"

Karo paused, shaking off the rain clinging to his fur. "They've always been here."

"In our lifetime, yes. I mean, before then. Imagine ... let the mind roam a bit."

"Hmm." Karo shuffled to catch up. "Don't be silly."

"It's only a thought, chap."

"Dangerous things those are"—Karo whistled—"dangerous things are thoughts."

Claude chuckled. "Hadn't thought about it."

They reached the crumbling timber staircase of the Drunken Monkey Inn. An undeniably dingy-looking establishment carefully crafted into a selection of old creeping trees laced with thick vines. In the current weather it seemed even grimmer than usual. Don't judge a tavern by its entrance, Father always said. You would never have a drink in Tierra Libre if that were the case.

They climbed up and entered quietly, avoiding the eyes of the weathered locals. The grizzled barkeep glanced up, poured Claude two mangolers and chucked a pack of saltesers at his chest.

Karo grabbed his tankard and downed half in a single swig. He wiped froth off his mouth. "This stuff is awful."

"Best they've got," said Claude, "and it won't stop you. Anyway, I wanted to ask you something. A little question that has been bothering me lately. Why did we ever join the SIs?"

"It's a bit late for me," said Karo. "For you, it won't be that bad. Although don't become one of those goblet-half-empty males like Dubbert Grouse."

"As if," scoffed Claude. "I'm not whingeing. It's a simple question. One you don't seem to be able to answer."

"What was the question again?" Karo asked, chomping on the salt snacks.

"Why did we choose Floor 9? And who decreed that we must *earn* a living? Who decided all these *rules* of life?"

"It is what it is," said Karo. "God of Work made the rules, and it all filtered down from there. Boring in some ways, yet needed. So we can all sleep safe and sound in our pods."

"What a life," Claude said, swiping Karo's beer mat. Putting it on top of his own on the edge of the table. With a flick, he flipped them, catching them in his hand. "Wouldn't it be funny if we all just said nah and quit?"

"Come on now," said Karo, looking around the inn. "Forget about the big stuff for a while. Let's see if we can find you a date."

Claude looked around too, unimpressed by what the place had to offer. Fierce, thick-set females talking too loudly. There were better looking monkeys on the other side of Hussleton's turnstiles, which was saying something.

"Sex is a powerful drive, Karo. But not that powerful."

His colleague laughed and wheezed. "Want another round?"

"Is our Holy One holy?"

Claude settled back into his seat as Karo waddled off towards the bar. By his calculations they could sink at least another two and still be back not long after curfew. *Right before the howlers get too vocal. I fancy another race home through the canopy.* The night at the Agumon had reminded him there was nothing quite like one of those beasts breathing down the nape of your neck to remind you that you still had a tail.

Karo returned with an anxious expression and plonked down two frothing banana beers. The cheapest pint on tap. The balding pichu took a gulp and leant into Claude with a whisper. "Barkeep said there's been some trouble in these trees. She wanted to check why we're here. Told her Monkey Business was the last thing we're after."

"What trouble?"

"Well, some treepers aren't happy." Karo snuffled a few more snacks. Claude snatched a tailful for himself before his friend ate the lot. "Unauthorised felling close to protected areas. Working conditions getting even stricter. State not supporting them in the way they should. And a few favourites got dumped in the Penitentiary on false charges, apparently." Karo gestured at the many grim-faced patrons of the inn. "Probably some idle moaning though—these monkeys don't have many brain cells to share around."

"My father's one of them," said Claude, feigning indignation.

He let the words hang. "So, did you come up with an answer? To my earlier question. Why we live such tiny lives?"

"We live within our means. Always progressing, Eyes Forward. As individuals and as a Tribe."

"Yes, they always drone No Monkey Business and Eyes Forward. But why?"

Karo huffed. "What do you mean 'why'?"

"Well, why only look forward? Why can't we look behind? Or down? Or up for a change?"

"Oh, you mean the actual direction. I said you're thinking too much about this."

"Come on," said Claude. "We could all look up and climb in the trees occasionally. Is that such a bad thing for a monkey?"

"We keep our limbs on the ground for the most part, it's the evolution of our species. Only treepers spend most of their hours above it."

"That's not entirely true, is it?" said Claude with a smirk.

"Enough," said Karo.

"I did tell you not to get me started." Claude hated being right all the time.

Karo appeared to grimace and held his chest. His face flushed as he gripped his drink.

"You okay?"

"I'm fine, just think we better finish up for the night." Karo sent another large dose of banana beer down into the depths of his chubby gut. They tilted their tankards again, emptying the last of the pints together, the official howler calls moments away.

"Okay, so what's your quick summary? After all your years of service, why do we live like this?"

"I said enough!"

Claude shrugged. "I'm only playing."

"No, it's dangerous. Real risky to get too far into this stuff. Upsets the balance of things. If a tree starts swaying too much, drooping too far, it's only going to end one way"—he made a savage gesture towards his throat—"dead on the ground."

"Crikey," said Claude, "what a heart-warming way to end the evening."

"Come on, I'm just looking out for a colleague. Let's roll."

"I wish."

"No Monkey Business tonight, please."

"Fine," said Claude, pushing his seat back and standing up. "Let's not do this again."

"You always say that."

"I do. Because you know your problem, old chap?"

"I have many, Claude. Which one are you referring to?"

Claude stepped closer, shook Karo by the shoulders. "You'll never break the rules. Never dream of it. Things will always be the same. Too scared to even take a fart in front of a hormiga. You'll end up in the village with a bad back, leaky gut and the rest."

"I do the best I can. With the life I'm given. Maybe you could take a leaf out of my book sometime. Might get a bit of peace for that restless monkeymind of yours."

"Doubt it," muttered Claude, and they both got up.

"I'd stay and have another drink if I were you," said a pichu who blocked the exit. She had small jewel-like eyes, a fortitude to them, with a collection of thin wrinkles. *A wise-looking monkey, this one. Clearly not a local. And her own patches of green …*

"We were just about to leave," Karo squeaked.

"I'd remain seated if I were you."

"We'll miss the curfew," Karo bumbled.

"There are worse things that can happen." Her eyes were on Claude. She tipped her tail in their direction before plunging down the inn's ladder in an exhibition of remarkably distinguished climbing skills for her moons.

The two pichus bickered, voices rising as they circled the decision. Claude leant back, arms crossed, waiting for Karo to tire of the back-and-forth. A smirk tugged at his lips. He knew how this would end. "Come on," he said, cutting through Karo's protests. He did not wait for a reply, already heading to the inn's balcony, bosky in hand, Karo close behind—his compliance aided by a round of moonshine brought out by the innkeeper, compliments of the stranger, apparently. Neither of them was one to look a gift monkey in the mouth, enjoying the special brew.

From their vantage point, Claude gazed out across the landscape. The Treetop of Valiant Ascendance loomed on the horizon, its highest branches reaching for the moon. Beyond lay the distant cloak of mist at the river's far edge.

A flash of red. Monkeys on the move. Fire torches illuminated a large rabble of them, at least thirty. Treepers—judging by their sturdy frames—climbing slowly north through the trees. Some carried homemade stakes in their tails, others gripped rusty felling tools. Something brought the mob to a halt. Muffled arguments broke out among those at the front, the words inaudible. The monkeys scaled their way down, coming to wait on the ground.

"This ain't good," shrieked Karo. "It's a peaceful petition."

"Might not be peaceful much longer," said Claude.

That was when they came, the howlers, fierce but in harnesses, led by a tall Acolyte and a horde of hormigas. The Acolyte barked something, and many of the treepers fled, scattering into the trees like sawdust at a felling. A collection held strong, closing ranks, facing the force in front of them. They pointed their stakes back, as threatening as they could. The Acolyte was talking animatedly with the hormigas. A cold indifference to his posture.

"What are they going to do?" Karo moaned.

"I do believe this is why she told us to stay inside."

The Acolyte blew a whistle and the howlers were released. Beside Claude, Karo cowered. He did not blame him, yet he could not look away. The beasts charged full pace at the treepers, covering the ground with great speed. High-pitched wails slashed the evening air. A few blows landed in defence, although they barely seemed to register on the thick hides of the howlers. Claude's stomach churned at the crunch of bones and horrible rip of flesh. He slumped forward in resigned acceptance.

Hormigas were sent in next. To rein in the hunters with their whips and ropes. They calmed the beasts and led them away, albeit still frothing at their mouths. Ready for their second dinner, no doubt. The rest of the hormigas remained under the watchful eyes of the Acolyte, picking up an assortment of limbs. Ruthlessly efficient.

It came fast and from the skies. A swarm of large vampire bats, eager for a taste of blood. The Acolyte seemed content to let the creatures feast. Claude wrestled his stare from the grim scene. *How can they get away with this? Fuerza and Tiarra would be turning in their graves.*

The mysterious monkey returned to the balcony, a stern expression across her brow. "I thought I suggested you stay inside?" A hint of despair too, maybe?

"We were about to—"

"It was my idea," said Claude. "We didn't expect to, um, witness that. Where were the law-keepers?"

"That's the wrong question," she replied. "What if the law-keepers are also the felons?"

"That was an Acolyte leading though, right?"

"Yes, the notorious Bain Longtail. Our Tribe's Head of Reality. Not a pichu you'd like to meet under a Red Moon. Or any moon, for that matter."

Longtail? I've heard the name before. "And what will he do now?"

"What the State is best at," she said with a dark expression. "Conceal things."

"Why would they be so stupid? Those treepers, they were

asking for trouble," said Karo.

"Because they want something," she continued. "Something is not right for them, and they felt compelled to challenge it. They want to protest, even if they can't articulate it fully. The most natural power of the Tribe lies within them, they just do not know how to yield it."

"And what is it they want?" asked Claude, intrigued by the candid words of the stranger.

"Freedom," she said with a flash of passion. "And they crave to find their voices."

"Their voices?"

"Yes." She looked wistfully back out from the balcony. Night had closed in except for the faint crimson glow of the moon. "There was a time when there used to be a real melody to this part of the rainforest. Songs rising into the canopy, voices of all different kinds blending together, floating harmoniously into the ether. Only those voices have been stifled, lost for a long time. Now we have a Monkey State by the few, for the few. But why should so few decide the fate of so many?" She swiped for a muddie. Catching it in her palm. "Anyway, you two really should be getting back to your pods."

"You said there were worse things than missing curfew." Claude flicked his bosky ash all the way down to the forest floor. "What might those be?"

She seemed to look at him closely then, an intensity. "Don't you know what curiosity did to the capuchin?"

"We do," said Karo, tugging at Claude. "We'll be on our way."

"We should share a moonshine sometime," said Claude.

"If Tiarra decides it so," she said with a nod.

A shuddering howler call focused their attention back on the time. The colleagues made for the staircase, Karo going first. It would take a while; he was not a natural climber.

As Claude clambered over the top, he glanced back. She was staring at the sky, cloaked in a strange mist that flickered around the vines of the Drunken Monkey. *One of those mogicians Mother told tales of?*

"I didn't catch your name?"

"I go by many," she said quietly. "But you may call me Joan."

"I'm Claude," he hollered back.

"I know who you are." The semblance of a smile. "Goodnight, Mr Talador."

Chapter Five

Holier Than Thou

The best leaders have vision and an unyielding strategy, but their most important skill is getting others to want to work for them. Once achieved, the worker is dependent on the authority and their compliance is locked in.

- Monkiavelli -

An almighty shower swept through Tierra Libre in true rainforest fashion. Claude's steps became a laborious trudge, his limbs sinking into the muddy ground, each lap a greater struggle to stay afloat. The rain pelted his face, blurring his vision, soaking him to the bone. The Commute, the archaic ritual, which always seemed a waste of time, now seemed utterly absurd in the face of the storm. Hundreds of pichus moving in unison, taking a set circular route, etched wider and deeper by generations past. The combined stomp boomed through the jungle, probably audible in Shadowbor even.

It was far too early to be doing this, too early for anything really. Why was sleep so denigrated? Something to be postponed or disregarded in favour of duty? Claude imagined staying in bed for a whole morning. Free of expectations and the same old schedule. Moments of stillness where time was not frivolously donated to the God of Work. But it would be considered the highest order of Monkey Business to even dare not rise at the morning alarm—rest was for the weak, for those who could not keep up with the demands of Tribe life. Apparently.

A memory nudged its way into Claude's mind: Sura and Cama, still tangled in the warmth of their bed as the soft light of dawn crept in. He and Tia would sneak in, trying to muffle their laughter but inevitably failing. They would lie there, curled against their parents, a tangle of limbs and sleepy smiles, no rush to get up. The only task was to listen to Sura's much-loved stories—tales of daring adventures ...

But that time was long past; the State had seen to that. He shook the thought away, attention now on the route ahead.

The Acolytes always led the way, their steps heavy and sure, leaving deep marks in the mud. Tia was no different. She hauled herself through with everything she had. He could see it in the tightness of her face—she was working hard. A bit too hard—her lips pursed, and a focused frown she probably did not realise was on display. She surged ahead, lapping the collection of stragglers—the older, infirm, depressed or fakers, left to struggle round alone. The townies were no better. Nearer the middle of the pack, faces passive, bodies moving, eyes empty. Lifeless even.

Why were they like this? Marching along to some silent, forgotten rhythm. Conforming without a word. *Because of her, that's why.*

He slowed his pace to peer at the Monvida. She lounged upon a carved bench, with plump cushions and pillows, on a raised platform in the centre, a roof held steady by four hormigas shielding her from the elements. The surrounding trees seemed carefully pruned, allowing a beam of light to shine onto her large frame, illuminating her patches of red fur as an almost prophetic being.

The Holy One indeed.

Claude smirked at the thought of her trying to do five laps in these conditions. She would not make even one. And who would dare carry her? Yet, as the sun peeked through the canopy, something struck him as … odd. His eyes narrowed, tracking the way the light fell. It seemed she cast no shadow. Not even a faint outline …

Something solid collided with his back. He pitched forward, faceplanted the mud. A gruff grunt from behind, followed by the heavy stomps of a large barrel of a townie trying to go past.

"Yeah, no problem," he snapped up at her. "Step on my head next time as well if you want."

She just grunted. Did not even look back or break stride. No doubt one of the turd-flinging monkeys from Floor 7.

Dripping with mud, Claude wiped off the worst of it. A splodge decided to settle right in his eyeball. Trying to clear it made things worse. *Brilliant. It never rains, it pours.*

He dismissed the offers of assistance from a few kinder

commuters, pulling his shoulders back as he rose from the ground.

Glancing again at the Monvida, her gaze met his, sharp and unblinking. He saluted back and returned to the task of moving through the quagmire, catching up with the slowest townies and soon falling back into the anonymity of the troop.

No Monkey Business. Today, at least.

***

Once at his cubicle on Floor 9, Beena groomed him with the affection of a loving mother, picking and prizing all the dried mud from his back. A welcome delay to the start of his work on the Minor Political Crimes Act.

Claude had nearly made it to lunch, thoroughly excited by the prospect of a bosky and some (almost) fresh air, when a hormiga with a long whip entered the space. They talked with Dubbert first, a serious expression from the hormiga, a grin from Mr Grouse. He then pointed straight at Claude.

The hormiga set off towards him in response. Beena flashed an anxious look; Claude offered a shrug. His first thought was to bolt for the lift—a race with a hormiga might be wonderfully entertaining, even more so than evading the howlers. *That'd give my dull colleagues something to feast on.* He remained seated though, deciding to spin on his cubicle chair instead. A look of utter disdain served up to his visitor.

"Mr Talador?"

"Guilty as charged."

"Is that mud on your tail?"

"Oh, no, no. It's the flies this time of year. Dreadful, you know."

"Is that supposed to be a joke, Mr Talador?"

"Clearly not. You're not laughing."

"Right," said the hormiga. "Well, as I'm sure you can guess, I'm not here for pleasantries. I've come to escort you to Head Office."

"I don't give a monkeys what you want to do." Claude yawned and put a hand to his mouth. "Wait! What did you just say?"

"The Head of the SI wants to see you. Now."

"In that case"—Claude sprang from his chair—"let's do this."

The whole office waited; curious heads peeked over the cubicle divides, others pretended to still be working, but the angle of their ears gave them away, tilted to capture every word. And who could blame them? The Head of the SIs was rarely seen or heard. Their existence only predicated on rumours of those lucky enough to spend a few moments with them, *or unlucky enough*, he remembered. For Claude, this was the most interesting thing to happen at work since his very first moon.

As he moved away under supervision, he sneaked in a couple of hops and skips, bringing uncontrollable laughter from some colleagues, gasps from others. Dubbert scowled.

A long series of steps took him down to what must have been close to ground level. A dusty passageway led all the way to a circular red door. A polished gold handle in its middle. He tried turning it, but it would not budge; a knock was greeted with silence. He bobbed about a bit, limbering up. Waited some more. Still no word. Eventually, as he was about to ask for further instructions, a powerful voice shot through his bones. "You may enter."

He pulled back the door and struggled to conceal his shock, rubbing his eyes. Sat behind a large rosewood table was the leader of the pichus. The Holy One herself. He had not seen a bigger monkey in the flesh. He stood, transfixed, powerless to look away from the vast belly area. The rolls of fat spilt out to each side. It was hard to conceive of her as a monkey at all. Hanging from trees. There would not be a branch that would hold her. She was supposedly great with a sword—swinging one of those would be hard enough.

Claude approached, praying she could not read thoughts. Up close, her face was almost intimidating—sharp, perfect teeth, prominent cheekbones and golden eyes that glinted with a deadly serious vibe. The deep furrow of her brow and the tilt of her head only added to the impression she was all work, no play.

With a single flick of her finger, a wisp of red appeared, swirling in the air, sending Claude stumbling directly into a seat in front of her.

His tail curled round the back of his chair as he settled.

"Name?" she barked.

"Claude Talador."

"Occupation?"

He rolled his shoulders, hands on thighs, sitting a little more upright. "State Inspector."

"Ever heard of a blade, Inspector?"

"Excuse me?"

"A fur trim?" Her features scrunched inward as she seemed to study him.

"I prefer the natural look, Your Holiness."

"Not very becoming of a townie, is it? But I guess we cannot control everything about our wonderful pichus."

Claude shrugged, resisting a wisecrack.

"Let's have a look at your report then." She huffed as she reached to the other side of the table, pulling out a pile of notes. Skimmed through pages of what Claude could only imagine was contained within.

"Hmm, interesting," she muttered, glancing through the dossier. "Quite the early academic record you have here. Although chose not to try for a more ambitious State position. That is unusual."

"Why, thank you."

"Not a compliment." She frowned. "An observation. So, tell me, with the unclipped tongue you seem to possess, does Floor 9 keep you occupied? And well nourished?"

"Well, the food is pretty bland."

"Go on."

She seemed a monkey who preferred it told straight. "I mean, it's lovely that the State provides food for the workers. Just a little repetitive sometimes. Especially the lichen rice. It's usually overdone, soggy and could certainly do with a dash of salt."

"I would not know. I do not eat it," said the Monvida. She grabbed a handful of assorted nuts and sent them straight down her gullet.

"Your sister works directly for me, correct?"

"It is."

"The two of you get on?"

"Occasionally."

"I see," said the Monvida. Claude could tell his every word was being assessed. "Did not fancy following her into the most noble of professions then?"

"Oh no, I wouldn't be seen dead in such a role."

"Is that so? You are an interesting-looking monkey, aren't you? Solid frame, keen eyes and those speckles of green … they come from which side of the family tree?"

"My mother's."

"And what does she do for a living?"

"She is no longer living," said Claude with a sudden coldness, bowing his head.

"Eyes Forward, pichu. I am sorry to hear that. There are few of your heritage left now, a shame really … What happened to her, if I may ask?"

"She was killed in Shadowbor."

The Monvida paused. She appeared to be weighing her words. A fierceness came to her eyes. "A terrible business really. Not a day goes by when I do not regret the loss of faithful servants in that Fuerza-forsaken place. She died for an important cause though, Talador. Never forget that."

What does she want me to say? Nothing can change the past.

"You still miss her, I can see." With great effort, she used her forearms to rise from seated to standing, moving to the one window. "I know how you feel. The pain of losing a loved one before their time leaves a scar that never truly heals. But, we must go on, bury ourselves in our business. Our day to day. Moon to moon. Work does not wait on sentiment alone." She settled back into her seat, grabbing a few roasted cashews.

None are offered across the table, I see.

"I will cut to the chase now, Talador. We have had a few reports of missed curfews at Dormor 43. A certain fervid member of the Tribe has reported some suspicious activity. Anything you would be aware of?"

"Nope." Claude cursed Dubbert again with the full force of his monkeymind. *The little blabbermouth!*

"Certain pichus arriving later to their pods."

"Beats me."

She looked at him with the face of someone who knew they were being lied to but did not see the value of challenging it head-on in the moment. "It is a shame when this sort of thing happens. Younger adult males often. They get a little bored. A little zealous for change. A little rebellious, one might say. It is all quite naive."

"Sounds it. We would not want monkeys to pursue change. I think—"

The Monvida slammed the table in front of her, and a small spark bounced and struck Claude in the chest, almost knocking him from his chair as the bowl of cashews went flying. Her eyes bored in on him.

Claude's mind buzzed with thoughts of escape; an invisible weight held him firmly in the chair. He also caught an unmistakeable waft of ferment. *Wasn't that outlawed during the working week?*

Her tone softened. "Do you know what I will command here?"

"No more Monkey Business." He shrugged.

"Yes, that. More importantly, though, I urge you not to indulge fantasies. Do not look to escape from your problems and hide your fears. You are one of the lucky ones; working in Hussleton, you represent the State. You have a higher purpose, honouring the name of Fuerza. Do you understand?"

"I do, Your Holiness."

"You will," she said. "The Tribe has real challenges right now, and it does not need cocky climbers like you getting ideas above their pods. Remember, any pichu is easily replaceable. I do not need you, yet you would very quickly find out how much you need *me*."

"I'll do what is needed for you, the SI department and the State." He got up from his seat and moved towards the back of the room. Claude reached for the door, only the knob would not turn.

"We are not done, Talador."

"I see," he said, jolting back round.

"I have something I want to put by you. I was thinking I have some work more befitting for a monkey of your intelligence." Slowly, her lip started to curl into its half-smile. "Put that sharp monkeymind of yours to work. A spot of secret service work, you might say."

"You want me to be a spy?"

"Oh gosh no, how uncouth. Just more personalised inspections, shall we call them, away from the office, more into the underbelly of the Tribe. Might be a bit more interesting than those reports you have been putting so much love into. I trust I can count on you?"

Claude looked at her. A roguish expression across her features. *It's pure Hobson's choice. One does not say no to her. Not directly, at least.*

"Of course." He smiled back.

"Wonderful," she said. "One of my Acolytes will be in touch shortly. Now be gone and may the fire of Fuerza be with you."

He made a hasty exit this time. Once outside the room, a barrelling wave of relief swept over him, like someone emerging from the State's Solitree after long nights without light or dreams. The hormiga with the whip stood alert and serious in wait.

"I'm alive!" Claude beamed, waving his hands, fingers splayed. Nonplussed, the hormiga beckoned for the route back to the office floor. "Any chance of a bosky on the way?" Claude added.

"You are to be returned to your cubicle, where you will receive further instructions."

"I'm only asking for one. A little break. I've not had my lunch—jojoba leaf sandwiches, freshly prepared chayote rice and extra guac. That was on today's menu, wasn't it?"

"Mr Talador, you are to be returned to your desk immediately. Please follow me."

"It's against Working Time Regulations surely?"

"Meeting with a Head of Department is not work, Mr Talador. Check the rules. I'd suggest you take your permitted break at a more suitable time."

"Golly, I'll just go hungry then."

"This way, please, and No Monkey Business. You'll disrupt the other workers."

As they returned to Floor 9, a hush fell over proceedings. Claude was escorted to his seat and sensed many eyes on him. He came to perch in his cubicle, grinning again. He gave a tip of the tail to Karo, performed a mock strangle charade at Dubbert, and glanced over to Beena with a wink. A second later, a wrapped bundle landed on the corner of his desk.

"Fuel," she whispered, lips barely moving. Claude grinned, snatching it up. A nutty bar speckled with grains of lichen. A little dry but delicious all the same.

A sharp whistle fired out, and they all went back to work. Eyes Forward once more.

Chapter Six

Day Of The Hundred

Rule 10 has caused pichus to question themselves. Fuerza said: "You must enjoy the fruits of your labour." The challenge arises when such celebration detracts from new projects. New missions of even greater importance. A modern monkey must temper this desire to indulge. They must maintain the ability to keep Eyes Forward. The progress of the Tribe is ever indebted to this hustle. To fully relax—wait till you have gone beyond the mist—with your family supported and your legacy solid. Only then, he says, is true rest deserved.

—From "Interpreting Fuerza's Twelve Rules of Work Efficiency" by Leif Gaia

Did it always start that way? Her rise to power had come in a fanfare of hope and expectation. Sharp of mind, strong of stature and puritanically perfect, she had embodied the ideals the Tribe craved. Back then, she had not seemed quite so … expansive either.

Her ascension had been sealed when she forced a yield from the ageing Monvida XXXIII in a sword fight that had been over faster than a vampire bat to fresh blood in the night. Her ordination paired with the Day of the Hundred, the anniversary of the genesis of the Tribe, a time when all pichus were allowed to return to their families for the day. Ordered more like.

For Claude, this meant a journey down south to the Shrouded Grove, where his father worked as a treeper, and a welcome escape from the stuffy offices of Hussleton.

Rather than climbing up the spiral steps that wound around the trunk of the family treehouse, Claude opted for the ageing rope ladder dangling at the side. It swayed under his weight, the fraying ends brushing against the bark. As he reached the top, the hum of the forest gave way to the faint sounds within. Tia clunking on the creaky floorboards, his father busy in the kitchen. He slipped through the side entrance, a gap in the panels that Cama had long since stopped patching.

"You could use the front door, you know," said Cama.

"I could," said Claude. "But where's the fun in that?"

He navigated to his customary spot at the head of the table, pulling out his chair, its legs scraping against the warped wooden floor. Tia sat to his left, surprisingly quiet, eyes fixed on a muddie crawling across a plate.

Their father entered the dingy dining room, a large tray wobbling in his broad hands; he plonked it on the table. Claude peered in. Bugslaw. The tang already teasing his nostrils. The crispy edges hinted at care, if not perfection. Tradition mattered to Cama. Even when it hurt.

"Three days this time," Cama said, gesturing to the dish as he settled into his seat. "Added a touch of chicle sap this year too. Thought it needed something … extra."

The trio sat in silence, eyes drawn to the placemat left out for the one who could not be there. Most monkey families would spend time grooming each other on such an occasion. Not the Taladors. Not anymore. For all the rituals of the Day of the Hundred, this was theirs now: a table that felt too large, a house that seemed too empty, memories too heavy to share aloud.

Claude reached for the ladle, breaking the spell. If they were going to sit in silence, at least they could eat.

Straightening in his chair, Cama spoke first. "We give thanks to the Monvida for the gifts we are about to receive."

"We give praise to Fuerza, the Holy One and those who came before her," said Tia.

"And we think of those departed," added Cama. "The time will come when we will see them again in the light beyond the mist, but for now, we keep our Eyes Forward."

They lifted their heads, picked up goblets of fermented fig wine and raised them in the direction of the tiny ornate box. A single green jewel on its front. Fireflies of dust dancing around it.

Claude turned to his food. The bugslaw was not crispy. It was burnt. He picked and nibbled at it anyway. As did Tia. What was the point in saying anything? He topped up their goblets with ferment, its sharp aroma triggering memories of evenings spent with both parents. He swirled his drink, far stronger than he remembered, but a reprieve from the underwhelming start to the meal.

Having cleared his own plate with brisk efficiency, Cama disappeared to the kitchen. Claude glanced at Tia, who was carefully rearranging what was left of her bugslaw, as though presentation might improve the taste.

When their father returned, he carried the main course with pride, a mixed nut roast and jackfruit fritters. A speciality in Tierra Libre, believe it or not. Claude filled his plate with little anticipation. One bite confirmed his suspicions, the lack of seasoning swiftly apparent. Tia nudged a piece of the roast to the floor. No doubt planning her next trip to the Forager.

"How's work in the trees?" Claude asked.

"As well as it can be," said Cama. "We've almost cleared the sawgrass all the way up to the Agumon in the south. It's long days, and we harvest the timber near the Tangle Tower. Each moon, the quotas get higher. Maybe you can do something for us, Tia?"

"I wish, Father. I'm afraid the State has many such requests. They can't all be answered. We moved towards privatisation for a reason."

"As you say," said Cama. "What's it been like working close to the Monvida?"

"It is an honour," said Tia, sitting up taller. "She's articulate, intelligent and cuts through any argument with logic. And when you talk to her, which I get to do on a weekly basis now, you can almost see the fire of Fuerza in her."

Claude chewed loudly, trying to distract his sister. It was unsuccessful.

She went on. "It's as if she's always one or two moves ahead of you."

What a load of howler dung! Claude almost choked on a sticky piece of jackfruit.

"Something funny, brother?"

"Oh, I was just trying to imagine our leader moving quicker than another pichu."

Cama chuckled, but Tia shot a glare back.

"Not that you're that far off these days, sister." Claude studied her ever-bulging frame without subtlety.

"Ever ahead of you though," she replied. "At last count, my aethersalt stack was triple yours."

"I'd rather create memories than accumulate salt."

"How's your SI work going anyway, Claude?" Cama asked, with a slow lowering of his palm at the siblings.

"So-so. Good days, bad days. I guess you could say I'm living the dream. Not far off the High Life."

The silence that followed suggested he had said something grave.

"Although, as a reward for recent good performance, I've been bestowed new responsibilities," he said, nodding at the table members.

"Do elaborate," said Tia with a smirk.

"I'll be conducting a series of private inspections as it happens."

"Reporting to who?" asked Tia, no longer smirking.

"Directly to my Head of Department."

"*You* met the Head of State Inspections?" Tia spat out some ferment and cackled. "Next you'll be trying to join me in the Acolytes."

I'd rather have a mango beer with the hormigas. "No chance."

"Wait, you might need a higher level of intelligence for that," said Tia.

Cama shook his head. "We all have our worth for the Tribe."

"More ferment?" said Claude. He received nods from the other two. Bouncing from his chair, he ambled to the kitchen. He filtered and strained more of the prangeo figs, unable to ignore the raised voices back at the table, and made a start on the washing up, delaying his return, looking forward to the pointless vigil being over.

He returned to the dining room, jug in hand, careful not to let any overflow.

Tia's enthusiasm bubbled as she delved into a new topic. "I've been particularly busy these past few weeks. The new Working Time Regulations are almost finalised. The Tribe will be switching back to a half day's rest. Still once a week, of course. The State feels that monkeys aren't using it enough. It's slowing brains down a bit. Have you heard about this, Claude?"

He extended the jug. *I could just pour this on your head.* "No, I've not," he said, pouring the ferment into her cup instead. *Karo's five-day-workweek petition went well then.*

Tia beckoned for a larger measure. "I think it'll be great for the economy. They think they will use it to increase logging efficiency. Then we can use the wood to build better offices in

Hussleton HQ. Hear it gets hot up there. And new living quarters for all the Acolytes in the TVA, naturally. How does that sound?"

Claude stuck his thumbs up. "Well, you know, as long as the Acolytes are well taken care of, what could possibly go wrong with society. It's not like there's a growing timber shortage or anything …"

"Pfft, don't believe everything you hear on Floor 9. There's still a great load of untouched bark in the East. Just sitting, waiting, for all our needs."

"Where exactly in the East?" asked Cama.

"The Holy One hasn't exactly gone into details. It's contingency. To be honest, I don't know why she doesn't order it all to be chopped down."

"We have to keep it sustainable," said Cama, quietly taking command. "I've chopped wood for more moons than you've both been alive. It's not as simple as hacking it all down. The best trees take an awful long time to flourish. Although I respect our leader very much, she does seem to have forgotten one of the most basic laws of the rainforest. For every tree you take down—"

"Another must be planted," the siblings murmured together.

"Interesting stuff," said Tia, trying to keep a straight face. He had seen her do it before—she always looked like that whenever Cama started one of his eco lectures.

"So, Tia," said Claude, leaning back in his chair, "please explain to me how exactly us pichus are supposed to welcome the fact we're losing a half day of rest?"

"There'll be some initial disappointment, maybe, but they know these things are well thought out. For their benefit," she said through a mouthful.

"How exactly is it for their benefit?" Claude pressed.

Tia surveyed the table, her own lecture brewing. "It's all about the law of scarcity. The rarer something is, or the more limited the supply, the greater the appreciation of it. You know how much you look forward to the day of rest after a long week of work? That will only be more exciting when you know it's just a half day. You'll value that half hugely." She looked at the other two, crossing her arms like she was the Tribe's Head of Law. "Through scarcity comes appreciation."

The ferment is going to her head. She clearly believes all the drivel being fed to her by the Monvida and those other sycophants in the TVA. My own sister, clueless.

Claude thought he would test her a little. "It doesn't sound that wise to me. What if the Tribe want to keep their full day? They give enough of their lives as it is. Everyone needs a rest. Why don't they go the other way? Give everyone two days' rest. Five days' work. That would mean the intensity of the work goes up. Rather than conflating tasks just because you're meant to be 'working'. Some ample breaks for play would help fuel a more effective workday …"

Cama smiled, seeming to appreciate Claude's more utopian vision.

Tia shook her head. "You just don't get it, do you? Smoking all that junk. Living with your eyes to the sky, never forward."

"I think you'll find I get it much better than you do," said Claude with a yawn.

"Really? Because you spend all day shuffling papers. Some of us actually have a real impact on society. Do real work."

"Yeah, making rules that harm your fellow pichus," Claude quipped. "If that's real work, be proud of yourself."

Tia leapt onto the table, sending plates crashing and the remaining ferment flying into the air, splattering the walls. She targeted Claude's throat; he braced for impact. They scuffled viciously, all limbs put to use, along with many attempted strikes of the tail. Cama shouted for them to stop.

They did not listen.

Tia unleashed a flurry of low blows, knocking all the wind from Claude. He retaliated with a well-placed elbow to her nose. She snarled, then managed to pin Claude to the ground, a glint of menace in her eyes, poised to smash his teeth out with her spare fist. Cama did not wait any longer, hauling Tia off. Red-faced and almost frothing at the mouth, she struggled to go back on the attack. It was futile though. He held strong.

Father has his uses still. Claude laughed as he dusted himself off. He left the table in disgust, disguising a limp, refusing to acknowledge the pain. He came to rest outside, hanging from the outer frame of the tiny balcony that offered views from the treehouse. As he rocked, his eyes were drawn to the softly shining Purple Moon that kept watch above the canopy.

There was only one option here. He had to get punk into

his system … and fast. He prepared his potion while looking out into the rainforest, the trilling of insects creating a wall of noise. They could not drown out the raised voices from inside the Talador family tree. He caught a few garbled comments from Tia. "The cocky gnat! He's depressed. Self-centred and rude. A disgrace to our fur!"

The hit from the wattsplant came, flooding his body with calm energy. Claude took victory in his greater control of emotions, a triumph that drew a smile. He savoured a few more puffs. As the punk began to take a greater grip, memories surged—the bird at the Agumon, the attack on the treepers, the conversation with the Monvida—and then further back, plunging into the recesses of the past.

She wouldn't have indulged in such petty squabbles. She'd sing to us instead, the most beautiful of tunes and tones. It always halted an argument. Claude thought of how she was said to have died. A vicious borderbeing mauling her to the ground. He fought the image away. It had been fifty moons ago, and all that remained were her ashes and memories fading fast.

"Son," came a whisper, which brought Claude back into the present world, "I'm sorry about your sister."

"She'll get herself into trouble one day with that temper."

"Yes, I have told her the same. She misses her too, you know. It's her only way to vent those feelings. Anyway, I understand she wishes to apologise."

"Ready when she is," said Claude, taking another puff of punk.

Cama paused before continuing. "Maybe she's not the only one who needs to forgive ..."

It was cooler out now, and the trees rustled in the air. The peace of night. Cama raised his tail back inside to where Tia was sitting at the dinner table, arms crossed, sulking.

His father put an arm around his shoulder. "Haven't got a little left for a hard-working old monkey, have you?"

Claude studied the monkey before him. Almost as broad as a howler, a strong and powerful frame that belied a weak will. A victim. Of his own making. Although, what did he have to fight for? Claude handed the punk to his father, who had his own pipe, and with a nod, Cama signalled for his son to leave.

Tia looked up as Claude approached. She sprang up, offering her tail. Claude took it and was ready to shake. Instead, she caught him in a vine-like grip, his tail locked. Stuck like a fly in a trap.

Tia smirked. "You know how much of an honour this is, don't you, brother, working for senior management?"

"Honour?"

"Just take it steady, that's all I ask. No Monkey Business."

Tia finally released him, taking a seat again.

I think the Monkey Business is just about to begin, sister. "Might as well finish off the ferment." Claude raised the jug aloft.

"I could be tempted."

"Wonderful."

They looked at each other for a moment then. Of the same blood but not the same mind. Still, they cracked goblets together, put them to their mouths and sent the contents down their gullets.

With a belch, Tia asked, "So where's your first gig?"

"The Dump."

"Wow"—she laughed—"quite the glamorous introduction."

Even Claude could not help but grin at this.

Cama returned to the dining room, contentment on his weathered face, a silent acknowledgement that his offspring were no longer at each other's throats. Yet, the true source of satisfaction might have been traced to the rare taste of rebellion he had just savoured—a fleeting indulgence for an ageing monkey who had spent a lifetime playing by the rules.

The three drank together for a while, talking of happier times and even regaling a few old songs. Lyrics long forgotten. What Joan might call a melody, maybe.

Chapter Seven

Huckster Of The Dump

*Most monkeys seem utterly unaware of their impact on the forest
around them. They cannot comprehend that they are part of
something larger. Interconnected beings, not solo climbers.*

—Adapted from "Ecosystems of Eldervaria" by Ede Nè

A strange feeling came over Claude as he neared his
destination. A new emotion. The sense that he was in the
right place, at the right time. Or maybe it was just a jolt of pure
relief from a life of perennial boredom in Tierra Libre. The
stench was overpowering, nevertheless, forcing him to hold his
breath while he hummed the tune of "Dancing Through the
Lunaforest". He moved on unperturbed, simply glad to be out
of the office. After two weeks of diligent work on Floor 9, he
had somehow passed the hormiga review and the Holy One
had been true to her word, sending him out for his first proper
inspection.

The entrance to the facility was guarded by two rough-and-ready towers and a weathered gate, the sign clear and imposing:

No Unauthorised Monkeys!

Claude could make out a pair of harsh eyes peering down at him from the windows of the closest tower. He stood upright and rang the bell.

"Who goes there?" came a gruff voice.

"It's Mr Talador"—he shuffled his badge—"State Inspector."

The monkey grunted. "Funny one."

"Seriously," said Claude, raising an eyebrow. "Open up."

"There's no deliveries today," said the voice. "We're not expecting anyone. Did you not read the sign?"

Service is shocking here. He waited another two ticks before ringing again.

"Who goes there?" the eyes asked.

"Mr Talador," he repeated.

"Not funny," said the monkey. "We've got loads of work to do today and these are stressful times."

Claude cleared his throat and switched tone. "I'm not sure how long you've been in this role but either you politely open this gate, look at my badge, and let me in or I go straight to my favourite Acolyte and get them to knock the damn thing down!"

An expletive and then hushed discussion came from the tower.

Another voice took over. "Why, of course, Mr Talador. We do apologise. We've had a spot of trouble with trespassers recently, so please be understanding. I'll let you in and give you the full tour myself."

Claude tried to see who had addressed him. "Many thanks, Mr …"

"Huckbane," said the older monkey. "Tom Huckbane. I'll be down in a second."

A wave of humid air hit Claude as the main gates creaked open, the rancid smell even more unavoidable. He wondered if the defences were less for keeping trespassers out, more for containing whatever mess was buried within.

"Welcome to the Dump," said Tom Huckbane, arcing his arms to present what was around him. He was a sleek middle-aged monkey, and his fur held an almost glossy tinge to it. Claude shook his tail and that of the guard, who then shut the gate behind them.

"Now for what do we owe the privilege of an SI on this fine day?" Tom asked.

"It's a standard inspection, Mr Huckbane, nothing to worry about."

"Why, of course. How can I be of service? And please, call me Huckster, they all do."

"Okay, Huckster, I need you to give me a full tour of the, err, facilities. Let me know what is going well and any challenges. I'll speak with your staff, go through some safety stuff, and we'll need to do a quick check of the accounts. Then back in Hussleton, I'll compile a summary, which will make its way to the Holy One, eventually."

Huckster cocked his head. "You think she'll read it?"

"I hope so."

"Well, I'm happy to help, Inspector. And I do trust we are in line for the five percent increase in funding this year?"

"In theory, yes. Unless she decides such salt would be better spent elsewhere."

"Understood." He waved over the returning grumpy guard, who passed them both a small wooden cup. It was warm to the touch and contained a blackish-brown liquid.

"Cheers, Dodge," said Huckster before turning back to Claude. "Apologies, it's not the best out here."

Claude took a sip, swilling it round his palate. "I've had worse," he lied.

Huckster grinned. "It's the air in these parts—messes with the beans."

"You chaps need anything else?" asked Dodge.

"No," said Huckster. "It's time we got cracking."

Once his colleague was out of earshot, he whispered, "That monkey's wanted out since he started here."

Huckster led Claude right into the belly of the beast. A hive of activity, noisy, with staff busy at work. Monkeys were moving all types of waste in the heat. Sorting what could be recycled and what could not. A few pedalled old trailer carts about the place, backing them up into vast trenches to cheers of delight.

"The Dump is home to some curious characters," said Huckster. "Many are former treepers after a steady wage. Take Eric, for example."

A dishevelled-looking worker ambled over—a body odour not to be described.

"How's life?" Huckster asked.

"Not good, boss." He grunted. "The wife's informed me she's leaving. All of a sudden like. Said I'm not bringing up pichlets with someone who constantly smells like shit."

"What did you say to that?" asked Claude.

Eric sniggered. "Told her I'm not that keen on bringing up pichlets with someone who looks like shit. But, hey, that's life in this Tribe."

Needless to say, Eric is now on the lookout for a new partner to pick the dirt from his fur.

After listening to more life stories from workers, Huckster took Claude to the outer perimeter of the Dump. Concealed underneath a few thick palms was an old structure. Its entrance had a reinforced door, which Huckster unlocked and heaved open to reveal a space. Full of stuff. Piles and piles of stuff. Stuff of all shapes and sizes. Crammed onto tables and shelves that bowed under the weight. In the corner was a solitary desk and lantern. There seemed to be no clear structure to what was put where in the room. An old, cracked gourd bowl sat next to a stack of woven palm-leaf mats, frayed at the edges; a box of crystallised bug eyes leant precariously against what looked like a snapped reed flute, its once-clear notes silenced forever.

Huckster seemed to know his way round though. "The not-so-secret stash," he said to Claude. "Where I store any prize goods.

After they've been cleaned up, of course, sterilised with lime paste."

"Thought it smelt better in here."

"Exactly. Amazing what you can do with a quick polish. I can sell some of it on the open market. Most of the profit goes straight in the State coffers, but I take a cut for us and the binmonkey who found the particular item."

Stacks of glistening salt sat piled in the corner. *No wonder they want to take a peek at Huckster's tax filings.* Claude made his way through the current items for sale. Unloved toys, battered furniture, muddy and stained accessories. *Looks like a load of old tat to me. Who would buy this?*

Huckster coughed. "One monkey's trash may be another monkey's treasure."

"I guess," said Claude, turning to leave the stuffy hideout.

But something tugged at him, drew him towards the desk. A thick layer of dust coated the cover of a striking old green book, *In Search of* माया faintly inscribed on the front in curling script, the name of the author worn off.

"Curious," whispered Claude, running his finger over the faded text. *I know that symbol . . .*

"Ah, yes, these kinds of books are a precious commodity these moons," said Huckster, plucking it from Claude's hands and moving it out of reach. He carried it to one of the shelves, retrieved a cloth, carefully wiped away the dust and flipped the book open to a page near the middle. "Freedom: the most fraudulent myth of the forest." Huckster looked up, clearly waiting for a response.

Is it even a myth now? "How much would such a thing set one back?"

"Depends who's buying." Huckster passed it back to Claude, an intensity to his expression.

Claude thumbed through a few of the pages himself. It was mainly tailwritten, the smell unique. "Just out of interest."

"Well," said Huckster, "I've learnt to let the potential buyer make the first offer. This lets you learn where their head is at right away. Made some great sales this way."

"I'd offer two grams of aether for this one. Hypothetically speaking, of course."

Huckster scoffed. "You'd have us out of business at those prices." He grabbed the book and placed it, standing up, alongside others of its kind. The book burning of Cindervale it seemed, had not been a complete success.

Dust motes swirled in the air as Huckster made his way back to the entrance. He paused, turned and faced Claude. "Not going to rat on a loyal State servant, are you, Inspector?"

"Course not." Claude lingered, eyeing the row of forbidden books.

"Wonderful," said Huckster. "I suggest we grab another coffee, and then I'll show you the real treat of this place. A sight you'll never forget."

"Can't wait."

"For the coffee?" said Huckster, chuckling as he pushed open the door. "Surely not. It's dreadful."

Truly dreadful. They both laughed. *At least this monkey doesn't sugar-coat the truth.*

As Huckster locked the door behind them, he became a little stern. "I don't think most pichus are aware of what happens to the waste they create. Out of sight, out of mind, maybe. Only, it must go somewhere. It doesn't just evaporate from the rainforest like rain on the roof. And that's our job—to manage it. To make it disappear. We do the best we can with the resources we're given." He paused, jangling the keys. "But if I'm honest, I'm not sure it's sustainable. Long term, that is. We could do with more funding, more support."

Claude nodded.

The foul scent greeted his nostrils again as they returned to the main part of the Dump, albeit less putrid than before. Clearly one got used to it the longer one remained in its presence. A bit like with a bad boss.

"It's a clearer picture this way," said Huckster, indicating for them to climb a steep path curving away from the main facility. Claude followed, ears catching the shouts and hollers of pichus toiling away behind him. The place was alive, in a manner of speaking. There were worse places to make a living.

"What hours do the staff do here?" Claude asked as they made their way up the slope, the incline enough to leave a faint burn in his limbs.

"Same as the townies," said Huckster. "Six days a week, six till eight. It's all physical, proper graft. Certainly need that day of rest when it comes. These monkeys are moving crap all day, every day. Literally. You smelt Eric." Claude had indeed. "I've lost three to broken backs, two with snapped tails, one with a nasty virus from a muddie trapped in their fur. All since the new Green Moon." Huckster shook his head. "Then there's Sammy. Poor lass was so tired after a busy week that on the day of rest, she didn't show up for worship. Didn't show up for her family meal. Didn't show up for work on the Friday. She's still knocked out in the Hope Wing of the Green Oasis, pure exhaustion. Can't even wake her."

The pain was clear in his eyes. *He cares for these monkeys. Like family even.* "I'm sorry to hear that, Huckster."

"Thank you, Mr Talador. She was a good worker to lose, and it was a sad time for our team. But don't go thinking we're a charity here. We enjoy the hard graft, the chance to be outside, using our bodies. It's what monkeys are made for, right? Although …" His tone dipped, bitter now. "My binmonkeys are paid a tenth of what those in Hussleton get. Some of the lowest-paid workers in Tierra Libre."

"Why's that?"

"You tell me, Inspector. I'm not saying any job is better than any other. What I can say for sure is this. If you took away all the binmonkeys, if we all went on strike tomorrow, the whole rainforest would be a festering cesspit before you could make your prayers to Tiarra."

Huckster's frustration was justified, but Claude had no

answers. He adjusted his speed as he continued to follow, the uneven route making the climb harder.

Almost at the peak of the hill, they came to a halt, both short of breath. The sounds of the workers below were already muffled. Before them stood the base of a ladder leading to what appeared to be an observation tower. An exceedingly tall one.

Huckster cupped his hands around his mouth and bellowed up. "Arabella!"

A rake-thin pichu clambered down the ladder, wary eyes flicking to Claude as she landed in front of them.

"Best eyes in the Tribe, this one," said Huckster, patting her on the back.

"Long distances, though, sir," Arabella replied with a shy smile. "Not so good up close."

"Arabella is our lookout," Huckster said, voice filling with pride. "Spends her days up here in the tower, watching over everything. Couldn't do without her."

"Nice to meet you, Arabella."

She glanced at Huckster, a blush colouring her cheeks as she ducked her head.

"She was a bit of a lost soul when I met her," said Huckster. "Took a liking to sneaking and stealing."

"I always returned the items," Arabella added quickly.

Huckster laughed. "That you did, Arabella. Even so, the Holy One suggested I let her join the staff here. Put her creativity to good use."

"Right," said Claude. *The State allowed that?* He had not expected Huckster to be on such good terms with the Monvida. "And you like it here?"

Arabella's eyes lit up. "I love it here, sir. Job suits me down to the ground." She paused, a mischievous grin spreading. "I mean, I prefer life off the ground, in the trees, but you know what I mean."

The three of them chuckled.

"It was my mah who taught me to be a sneaky monkey. I can get into most places without being heard. I bring things for the boss's secret stash. He makes me return them too, most things anyway."

"What does your mother do?"

Her smile faltered, head drooping.

"She's in the Pen." Huckster wrapped a protective tail around his ward. "Why don't you take your break a little early, Arabella?"

"I've still got two hours to do."

"Consider it a special treat. Two hours' break rather than one today. I need to take the inspector into the Nest."

"Two hours?" she chirped back.

He waved her away. "Go help the others if you get bored."

She did not need to be told twice. She beamed, bowed gracefully, then turned and charged off down the slope. "Nice to meet you, sir," she squeaked over her shoulder.

"Nice to meet you too," Claude replied, but she was already too far away to hear.

Huckster had his sterner expression back on. "Right, the ladder is a little rickety, so take it steady. I'll go first, and once I hit the top, I'll call down. Step forty-two is missing, just so you know, best to count your way up on your first go."

With that, the leader of the Dump shot up, clambering into the tower with ease.

A seasoned climber, I see.

"What are you waiting for?" shouted Huckster.

I bet he thinks a townie like me will struggle with this. He doesn't know Claude Talador.

Claude leapt straight up to the highest rung he could reach, gripping hold and propelling himself upwards. The climb roused something inside, as if his bones ached for it. He clambered over the top and landed with a low thud, entering a pokey hutch with timber floorboards, a low table and two seats over by a canopy window.

"A nest indeed," said Claude.

"Yes," said Huckster. "Arabella is convinced she's seen a bird from up here. Black feathers, rainbow-coloured beak, hence the name. Her friend only comes when she's calm, apparently, never when I'm around. Not seen so much as a feather myself."

Claude said nothing, his attention drawn to the table instead. Scattered across it were tail-scribbled drawings. Impressive in their detail. He reached for one.

"I would've moved those," said Huckster, hastily gathering a pile and covering it, "had I known you were coming. It's a quiet role for Arabella most of the time, and she's got an active monkeymind. I encourage her to draw as long as she keeps an eye on what's going on down below."

"They're brilliant," said Claude, clutching an image of the Monvida in all her regalia and a frown. "Quite expressive." A deep red colouring on the chest.

"If you must know"—Huckster shook his head—"not all the pieces are Arabella's. A few, like the one you're holding, were drawn by a much poorer artist."

Claude suddenly twigged. "You draw too?"

"Guilty as charged. It helps me think outside the box a little. Worry less about my team and how we're doing."

Art was rare in any form. Not outlawed. But certainly not encouraged. It would be borderline Monkey Business in this day and age. Yet here was Huckster. A leader who could draw, could read, could climb. Could think for himself even. Claude felt a flicker of admiration for the pichu before him. *He's no blind follower of the established order.*

"Do you draw?" Huckster asked.

"Never tried."

"I see." Huckster paused, seeming to be weighing his words. "If you don't mind me saying, you don't seem like a standard inspector, and I don't just mean your fur. Some say the Tribe lost its capacity to think a long time ago. Ordinary monkeys gave up on what it meant to explore the world around them. Forgot they could lift their eyes upward, as well as forward, once in a while. I sense this is not the case with you." He looked back at the depiction of the Monvida. "I'm glad you can appreciate an interpretation, despite its limitations."

A wry smile emerged. "It's art. That's the whole point." He put the piece down. "I used to sing a bit myself. I guess that could be called my art. Although it's something I'd keep confined to my pod."

"What a shame," said Huckster. "We also never take the work out of the Nest. We know they're not things normal pichus would want to see. The work itself is a release, though, a chance to go outside yourself, an escape. One that's needed here." He gestured to the window. "And I guess now you'll see why …"

Claude had momentarily forgotten why he was even here. He snapped back to attention, making his way over. They had really come up high, at bird's eye level, for sure. The air felt different, cooler, purer. The faintest tickle of a breeze.

Holy Mother of Fuerza!

His heart sank all the way to the forest floor. Piles and piles of waste littered the ground, a sprawling mass of refuse that stretched and bulged. A thick grey smog emanated from the site. A living entity, choking the air and bleeding into the horizon.

No birds would dare venture here.

Chapter Eight

Report In

The Verdan Emeral will reside alongside us. Unintentionally,
covertly. Not ordained for greatness but blessed with an inner resolve
and outward power that will, in time, reveal itself. The wait may be
long. Times may be hard. Yet the light of Tiarra will shine again.

—From "The Book of Moons" by Imani Zinn

The morning after his inspection, Claude shot straight to
Floor 9. Energised by his first day outside Hussleton, he
was keen to write up what he had witnessed from the Nest. The
rotting, ever-growing pile of waste was almost bursting out of
the facility. Pichu consumption was far outstripping the available
forest. Huckster's monkeys worked hard, but they were being
pushed to breaking point. In his report, Claude made sure to
stress that the State was probably not aware of the problem—
or certainly its pressing nature. He scanned the office full of
paper-pushing monkeys, the recycling bin itself overflowing. *The
timber shortage clearly doesn't extend to Hussleton.* He had also been

asked to report on the character of the owner of the Dump. Writing about Tom Huckbane brought a smile to his face, and he signed off a report of absolutely No Monkey Business on site.

"I've never seen you like this," said Beena from the next cubicle. "How was your first day?"

"Not right now," he said, tailwriting an introduction on the dangerous state of affairs. At the bottom, he highlighted that an increase of ten percent in funding would be advisable. This would go towards staff welfare, better waste carts and an innovative recycling method under development.

The whistle blasted out that almost sent Claude flying off his chair, just about gripping on. Looking up, he saw Beena smiling. "It's good to see you like this. Maybe you've found your calling?"

"Steady on"—Claude glanced back at his report; it needed more work, but some hope stirred—"let's see what action comes of it first."

Before Beena could respond, Karo bustled over, dark circles shadowing his eyes.

"You seen the news? Absolutely preposterous! No consideration for us loyal townies. One day, I swear, I'm just not going to turn up, like you said, chap, and shove their workload where the sun doesn't shine—"

The other two pichus exchanged a glance, both lowering their arms at him. Across the room, Dubbert Grouse was sniffing about, expression eager for the latest gossip.

"The sun doesn't shine here much anyway," said Claude,

nudging Karo, "but what's got your tail in such a twist?"

Seething, Karo thrust a document right in front of them. "Preposterous," he said again.

Claude took the press release, and Beena leant in, reading over his shoulder. It brought a gasp from her but a grimace from Claude.

> *Update To Pichu Law*
>
> *As of tomorrow, the day of rest will officially be shortened to a half day, six hours to be precise. There will be no Commute; however, monkeys will be required to work from the hours of 8 a.m. to 2 p.m. A whistle will sound to mark both points. The hours of 2 p.m. to 8 p.m. will be free until the usual curfew. If you'd like to learn more, our Head of Reality will be holding a lecture to explain the rationale behind the decision. It will support the continued progress of our State. Any questions in the meantime, please contact your nearest hormiga.*
>
> *Eyes Forward.*

"What a load of howler dung," muttered Claude. "Bosky?"

"No, you chaps go. I've had my break already." With a beckon of her tail, Beena said, "Let me check over your report, Inspector. I'll whip it into shape."

"Deal," said Claude, already bundling Karo towards the lifts, while Dubbert swooped over to question Beena.

***

The pair loitered in the rejuvenation area. There was nothing rejuvenating about it. The stools were hard as trunks. The water cooler was broken—again. And Karo was a monkey in a mood.

"They blooming well ignored our five-day-workweek petition. Now this!" Karo threw his arms up as he paced. "How am I meant to balance the demands of full-time work and a young family? Bo says I need to think about a side hustle too. Top up our pensions. It never ends!"

Claude's eyes began to glaze over, as did his ears. *I've heard it all before. I've a certain amount of pity, for sure. Karo deserves better. But he'll do zilch about it, as usual …*

"What if you just quit?" Claude threw out there.

Karo stopped pacing. "I beg your pardon, chap."

Rising from his stool, Claude moved to face him. "What if you handed in your notice? Gave yourself some time to properly work things out. Find work away from Floor 9 …"

A frown crossed Karo's face, but the tension in his shoulders seemed to ease. "I mean—it's not impossible—it would reduce the stress. Give me a chance to think. But Bo would think I'd gone bananas. We don't have the disposable salt. I can't imagine what I'd do instead. There's—"

A soft cough interrupted them; both turned as Beena poked her head into the room. She had probably been there for the entire monologue. "Sorry to interrupt, but someone wants to see you, Claude."

Claude left Karo mid-thought and returned to his cubicle.

A hormiga lurked there. In *his* chair, rocking side to side.

"The cheeky git," Claude whispered as he made his way over. "Excuse me!" he said much more loudly on arrival.

The hormiga stopped rocking. "Mr Talador, taking another long break, were you?"

"And who are you?" said Claude, both eyebrows raised.

"I'll take that as a no then." The hormiga noted something down on a clipboard before getting up from the seat.

"Thank you." Claude reclaimed *his* cubicle, sliding into *his* chair, swinging one revolution, two, three, coming to a stop before a fourth. "You can inform your boss that I've been working very hard on the first assignment." He looked at Beena, who gave him a small thumbs-up. "And I'm, err, just finishing it up now."

"Excellent, Mr Talador. Pass it over as is, thank you."

Claude cleared his throat. "It was a figure of speech." He needed to play for time. "It's not *done* done. A few final tweaks required. You know how it is?"

The hormiga tilted their head, studying him for an uncomfortably long beat. "Okay, Mr Talador, I shall wait with you here then until it's ready."

"Ever heard of a bit of personal space? Or patience?"

"Yes. Monkeys like us are trained in patience, something that certain weaker pichus seem to lack."

Wow. "Hear that, Maitri. Us townies, weaker monkeys we are. Maybe we should retrain and become hormigas."

Beena was clearly trying hard to stifle a giggle, but a tiny snort slipped out, earning her a glare from the hormiga.

"And what's *she* got to do with it?" they asked, turning, and inspecting her cubicle.

"I have a name," said Beena, rising from her seat, report in hand.

"Which is irrelevant to me." The hormiga moved closer to her, gaze settling on the document she held. "Not doing Mr Talador's homework for him, are you? That's very sweet. An old washed-out monkey taking pity on her colleague."

The insult landed like a slap. It took a moment to register, but when it did, anger fired through Claude's system. He shot up from his chair, bounced from his cubicle, squaring up to the hormiga. "Stop right there, you little snake."

"Leave it, Claude," said Beena, thrusting the report into his hands and sitting back down with a huff.

Claude gripped the pages. "If no one flicks away these ants," he snarled, eyeballing the hormiga, "soon they'll infest the place."

The State servant looked unfazed. "The only infestation here is you two," they said. "Sat on your tails all day, banking your aethersalt and shuffling your papers. And might I remind you—it's me who will be delivering this report to the Head of Department. So if you want this"—they tapped the document with their clipboard—"ten percent increase for the binmonkeys, I suggest showing a little more respect."

Two more hormigas scurried over. One held a blade, the other a whip. A hush fell over Floor 9. Dubbert was out of his cubicle, edging closer. The hormiga with the whip struck. Two sharp cracks echoed through the room, slashing down on either side of Claude—close enough for the sting of displaced air to brush against his fur. A muddielength and they would not have missed.

Point taken.

Slowly, deliberately, he slunk back into his own chair. "Send in the clowns," said Claude, defiance lingering despite his retreat. "At least give me a proper day to do a proper job."

"One moment, Mr Talador," said the lead hormiga. He took the other two off to the side. Forming a huddle. They covered their mouths as they spoke. Beena flashed a look over at Claude. He performed a long, drawn-out yawn.

The lead hormiga returned, posture stiff and self-important. "Tomorrow morning, Talador. No later. Or I'll personally drop your badge back to the State."

Claude waved him away. "Yes, little one. Don't lose sleep over it. You'll have it by noon."

"Very well," said the hormiga. They pointed at Claude's badge and imitated the prospect of ripping it off his neck and throwing it in the bin.

"Have a good evening, sir," Claude added with a wink. "Got something nice planned for the day of rest tomorrow?" A sharp shake of the head was the hormiga's reply. "Sorry, the half day of rest. So kind of you to cut our free time even further."

"We don't need rest, Mr Talador. Enjoy yours though. You clearly enjoy having no purpose and offering little benefit to your

Tribe." The hormiga's tone was almost gleeful. "Just get the report done. These games you play could quickly get tiresome …"

"If this is your idea of a game, you really need to get out more." Claude laughed. "Catch you tomorrow then."

"No Monkey Business," the three hormigas bleated in unison, scurrying from the office.

As the door swung shut behind them, Claude leant back. His victory, as small as it was, felt deserved. But a drawn-out exhalation from the next desk drew his attention. Beena was hunched over, tail too still, a little too focused on her work.

"Don't let those *things* get to you," said Claude. "They've got no power."

"It's not that," she said, looking up but unable to meet his eyes. "Don't worry about me."

Claude was already by her side. "What's up?"

"Oh, I don't know. What if they're right? Maybe I *am* just a washed-out townie. I've been here longer than any of the furniture, including that darn fan! Look at me. I never do anything out of my comfort zone."

"We freed those butterflies," Claude suggested.

Her mouth raised in a hint of relief. "That we did."

He remembered the night well. With Sura's help, they had snuck into the side entrance of the butterfly emporium. Opening most of the cages. Before the guards came. The Monvida had apparently been furious. But the sight of the colourful creatures filling the sky had been well worth the risk.

"And remember, you chose this line of work," said Claude, pointing around. "You always wanted to be an SI. It made your parents proud, right? You tried coffee bean counting on Floor 7—you hated it. You tried working outside, hated that even more. You do an excellent job, right where you are."

"That's not it, Claude." Beena's voice wavered. "I've done alright, put in the moons. I do like the pichus here, most of them anyway. But what I've never told you, never told anyone in fact … is that I regret my decision to become an SI every day. I regret it every single morning I pass through those turnstiles." Beena slouched over her workspace, shoulders curling inwards, elbow knocking over her water. The spill crept across the desk, dripped off the edge. "Oh well." She sighed, dabbing at the puddle.

Dubbert's nose was already out of his cubicle, twitching like a scavenger sniffing out scraps. Leaning in now, ready to pounce. Claude's tail shot out, a silent warning for the nosey tattler to stay put. He did not have the patience for Dubbert's antics, not today. Message received, he turned back to Beena, placing an arm around her.

"Beena, you provide well for your family. Your colleagues respect you, rely on you—me most of all. That's got to count for something, surely?"

She raised her head, eyes brighter, and her tone softened. "I guess that's true. Their father isn't qualified for anything, so I've had to do it. To give the infant a proper upbringing. All of it."

"Exactly," said Claude. "I'm proud of you, anyway. Got me

through my first moons well enough. Kept my spirits up through the drizzle. If only you were a couple of moons younger, Beena, I'd sweep you off your feet and propose under the next Blue Moon."

"More like two hundred moons younger," she said, unable to conceal a smile. "You could have almost any female in Hussleton, what you waiting for?"

A brilliant question, my lovely colleague.

"I don't want a townie. They're all stuck up. Boring as a hormiga. Except you, of course, you're great."

"Shush now," she said, swatting him lightly, "you'll make me blush. But you know my views on this. You need to find yourself a nice career pichu. Someone to settle down with."

"And where exactly would I find one of those?"

She tapped her chin. "What about Giulia?"

"Too boring." He rolled his eyes dramatically. "So boring she'd put me to sleep in minutes. Although, maybe that'd be a good thing …"

Beena tilted her head towards the desk nearest the toilet. "Karen?"

Karen V sat there, dabbing her cheeks with powder, a perennial pouter. And an office gossip up there with Grouse. Claude laughed. "Come on now."

"Oh, I don't know." She was already running out of options. "Gladys is recently single. She likes to go to the nutball games. She could be—"

"Don't be ridiculous." He tutted, knowing *exactly* why

Gladys Thickfur was single. "I have got *some* standards, you know. I need someone a bit different. Someone exciting. Someone with dreams. I'm attracted to female monkeys, not those born of that genetic composition but spend all their moons trying to be the opposite. I want a free spirit, one who can climb, one who can sing, one who can—you know—live a little …" He looked wistfully around the office full of busy worker bugs. "Such a soul lives only in my imagination, I fear."

'Cause they sure don't exist here.

Chapter Nine

Harsh As Punishment Goes

What if what you thought was your future had already occurred?
What if the present wasn't fixed so firmly to the now, but instead
bent and stretched like shimmering light near a star? Imagine your
life's journey unfolding not in a straight line but in curves and loops.
They say it's impossible to defy the arrow of time. They are wrong.
We do it every day—drifting through minds that warp memory and
possibility, venturing into distant futures and falling into blurred
pasts. Where will you spend your precious time …

- Nolan van der Linden -

Claude left the Commute at 5:15 a.m., taking the rare opportunity to climb through the trees out east. A long way east. He went through the backstory in his monkeymind. Crime in Tierra Libre was at an all-time low. This appeared to be a positive on first analysis. However, as Beena had explained, the reality was more complicated. A staggering amount of funds had been poured into developing the Penitentiary. Numbers in there were relatively low, an inefficiency the Monvida was keen to address. Her solution? The creation of new crimes. Claude snorted. The logic grimly elegant. The more crimes defined, the more treepers could be convicted—a fresh influx of monkeys for the prison. The beauty of this was that the Penitentiary was responsible for around sixty percent of the Tribe's manual labour. The type of pichu that fell afoul of the law was not often the brightest but often burly. Usually male and ripe as a fresh mango for hard physical work.

He shook his head. *Crime as a recruitment strategy.* It was hard to tell if it was genius or callous. Probably both.

The trees began to thin, and the view ahead shifted. A sprawling complex shrouded in mist. The Penitentiary. A huge outer building, the wooden staked walls at least twenty pichulengths high, stakes brimming with luvé power. Less of a gateway to the East, more a fortress. Its imposing presence dared anyone to challenge it. Or enter it even.

Outside the fences, a grey-tinged pichu tended to a garden. He moved among the plants and foliage, a calm way about him, watering yellow vanilla orchids, red betel nut palms and green fiddle-leaf figs—a small space of vibrant colour, more colour than in the whole of Hussleton.

Claude coughed, and the gardener paused, finishing tending to one flower, a stunning specimen of orange and purple with a beak-like head. Holding the stem with what seemed like reverence, he whispered something, and without a word, pointed to the prison entrance. He turned and looked at Claude, gaze lingering briefly before he tipped his head and turned his attention back to the abundant coconut palms that lined the edge of the patch.

Claude watched for a moment. He could not put his finger on it; there was something different about the monkey. When his fur caught the light … *I spy a few patches of red among his grey.* Not bright, but a hint. The glow of embers hidden beneath ash. *An old pyromancer, maybe?*

Shaking off his curiosity, Claude moved to the entrance, resolving to look out for the gardener again later.

Four hormigas converged on him, their brisk efficiency leaving little room for pleasantries as they checked him into the facility. One took a good sniff of his satchel, raising an eyebrow. Claude tapped his own nose in response. *Breathe. Relax.* He had not packed his punk on this assignment.

The hormigas moved aside, letting him pass, and escorted him to a sheltered entrance hall where a polished revolving door waited. One gestured for him to go through. Claude took the invitation. Too good an opportunity to miss. A smirk and he pushed off, whizzed round—twice for good measure. The world tilted as the door spat him out, and he stumbled into the foyer. *Smooth, Talador. Real professional.* He wobbled his way to reception area. Doubted anyone would have noticed.

"We've been expecting you," said a wiry pichu seated at a glossy teak table piled high with neatly ordered papers. His glasses slipped down his nose as he peered over them at Claude, expression nearly neutral. He uncurled a limp tail and extended it.

"You're earlier than we expected."

"Keen to get started."

"Impressive, Mr Talador," said the receptionist, straightening an already perfectly aligned stack of papers. "If you'd just like to take a seat, my colleague will be with you shortly."

It had barely been two breaths when a brash monkey came bounding towards him.

"Officer M Mantel," she said, offering a more vigorous shake than her colleague. "Mants will do. You'll be wanting coffee? Long trip and all. We've got the freshest beans in Tierra Libre, even out here by Easthaven. Best I've tried, in fact. Then let's get to it. I'm not one for hanging around."

Before Claude could respond, the receptionist shuffled out, placing a steaming mug of coffee beside him. He lifted it. Did not even manage his first sip.

"In fact, let's move and talk," Mants said. "You can bring that with you."

"Sure," said Claude, rising. "I've got a number of questions I'd like to run past you, Officer."

"We love those," she said, doing a little mock roll of her fists, "we really do."

True to her word, Officer Mantel fed Claude with a constant supply of statistics, achievements, operational insights, punctuated with caffeine hits—all delivered with the efficiency he associated with the State's finest. She was exactly the kind of pichu the State loved: organised, diligent and extremely committed to the cause. Exactly the sort of pichu he hated. Claude concealed his thoughts with a stock smile and a barrage of sensible questions.

Veering off the main compound, they passed a box-like library—its shelves crammed with State-controlled literature. The dull, utilitarian covers bore titles he recognised immediately; propaganda-laced accounts of Tierra Libre history.

They navigated through a narrow passageway into a darker part of the Penitentiary. Caution marked both their movements as they reached a series of dingy cells. The air held a stuffiness, and a whiff of urine assaulted their senses. Wrinkling his nose, Claude placed his tail to it. *And I thought the Dump smelt rotten.*

"They call it the Nuthouse," Mants said. "The Centre for Distressed Minds, officially."

Claude's eyes adjusted to the dim light. Each cell was little more than a grimy cage. "For those struggling with their mental health?" he asked, peering into the nearest one.

"Precisely, although struggling would be an understatement, they're—"

A harsh cry erupted from further down the chamber. The figure lunged at the bars, rattling them with surprising force. The monkey poked a dishevelled head out, arcing it round towards them, sunken eyes boring into Claude.

"Let me out!" he bellowed. "I have to go back!"

They moved closer. The pichu looked deranged, congealed spittle clinging to the fur around his mouth.

Mants went right up to the bars. "I've told you, John, you stay here until you're safe to be in with the others."

"You don't understand!" John's claw-like hands darted through the bars, aiming for her neck. His fingernails, yellow and gnarled, swiped the air, missing. His wild eyes shifted, fixing Claude in a stare again. "You! Let me go East!"

Mants did not wait; she shoved the monkey back, sending him sprawling. John yelped and collapsed to the ground. Cowering in the dark cell. Retreating into the shadows.

"What are you talking about?" asked Claude.

"Leave it," said Mants.

John scrambled forward on all fours. "You don't know? Do you?"

"Know what?"

"The damn lies they feed us." John let out a throaty laugh. "The great illusion. There's a whole world outside our—"

"Enough!" ordered Mants just as two hormigas arrived. They opened the cell, descended on John, pinned him to the ground. The struggle was brief but fierce, screams muffled as they forced him to ingest something.

His body wilted, his expression vacant. The eerie quiet that followed almost deafening. Except for the rasping breaths of the other inhabitants.

Mants exhaled sharply. "We don't have time for this nonsense."

A tremor went through Claude as they departed. The monkey's words still ringing in his ears. "East?" he asked Mants when they reached lighter surrounds. "Why would he possibly want to go there?"

"Beats me," she said. "You wouldn't catch me climbing the

other side of Easthaven. Thought of those borderbeings gives me the creeps."

Claude's intrigue was not satiated. The way John had spoken, the conviction in his voice. The monkey had been adamant—hard to ignore. "What did he mean about going back?"

"No idea." She shrugged. "John's just some strange monkey who evaded justice for a load of moons. All he does is jabber on about the East, some imaginary waterfall and a place ... I forget the name of ... Anyway, I think now you get why they call it the Nuthouse."

You're not wrong, Ms Mantel, you're not wrong. As they kept moving, another thought crept in. *What if he had made it out? What if John's saner than the lot of us?*

***

Claude waited in another part of the facility, ready for what Officer Mantel described as a "routine punishment for the Pen".

The monkey they brought in was wasting away, fur receding, with patches of chafed skin on show. Two hormigas carried him between them, his frail frame sagging like a cracked branch. They placed him in a chair positioned in front of a pool of water. A strange smell hung in the air. *It's the withered pichu.*

The guards strapped the monkey in as he sat, offering no resistance, and checked the tightness of the bindings before stepping back, standing as still as sequoias. Mants gestured for Claude to head out through a doorway and close it behind him. He entered what seemed to be an observation room. A wide bamboo-panelled window had a table and chairs behind it. Unsure what to expect next, he sat down.

Mants spoke quietly with the hormigas. The bedraggled pichu had mainly been looking at the ground. He now fixed his eyes on something else. Claude. A pleading look. A silent cry for help, maybe.

Claude swallowed hard. It was just protocol, just another task. But the way those eyes bored into him made him wonder. *What exactly do they consider "routine" in this place?*

"Are there any words you'd like to put on record?" Mants boomed at the pichu. "An apology to the State?"

Initially, the pichu shook his head. "Wait," he said, voice wavering. "I guess I'd like to say sorry. To my family, I love them."

Officer Mantel's expression did not shift. "I'm sure they'll be consoled." She ordered a hormiga to scribble down notes.

Fidgeting in the observation room, Claude struggled to ignore the growing tension in his chest. Officer Mantel, with a strange glint in her eye, signalled for the two guards to proceed. She whispered a few words before moving away.

Claude could not avert his eyes. The resignation of the pichu in question had turned to fear, his bedraggled frame shaking. The guards hauled him out of the chair, keeping his arms and legs tied. They then hoisted him over the dark pool. Holding him above it.

No way! A hot flush flowed through him. He looked desperately round for Mants. She was nowhere to be seen. The guards forced the pichu to kneel while bound a muddielength from the water. Teetering just above the surface.

With a brutal shove, the guards thrust him down headfirst, gripping his legs. The pichu writhed and fought under the surface. A primal response, a desperate action. His breath fading fast. Oxygen nowhere to be found.

Claude's own heart bashed against his ribs. "Hey!" he shouted. "You're going to kill him!" He lunged towards the bamboo mesh, banged on it with both hands. "Stop!"

The guards did not listen. Or could not. They were just doing their job. Just following orders.

Frantic now, Claude scanned the room, seeking an escape. He rattled the door. No joy. She had locked him in. He pressed his nose through one of the window panels.

The pichu was being wrenched out, somehow still alive. Clinging on.

Thank Tiarra.

Officer Mants tapped him on the shoulder. "Satisfying, isn't it? The Rule of Law in action."

"You're letting him go back inside, right?" Claude glanced again at the prisoner, who was swaying even under the hold of the guards.

"Oh no. This monkey's no longer a pichu. By law, these are his last few moments in the Tribe. Well, in life, actually." She pointed back to the scene. "You're going to miss the best bit."

A desperate thrashing from the legs. Intense concentration from the hormigas. They fought to keep the pichu submerged. A horrific gurgle came from the water.

Then nothing.

The body went limp; the guards released their grip.

It floated to the surface. A methodical checking of his pulse.

"Forgot you haven't seen one of these before," chirped Mants. "You get used to it, all part of the job. And that former treeper, well, let's just say he deserved it. Now, let's go get you some fresh coffee. I'll show you to your workspace. So you can crack on with your reports."

Claude nodded, not really registering what was said. His eyes were back on death row. The old gardener was inside, shuffling, head downcast.

A harsh whistle blew out.

"Come with me," Mants said without waiting for an answer.

They hurried through the main prison, the shouts drawing them closer. Two inmates, fur matted, were locked in a violent scuffle. Limbs and tails swiped through the air. Not pretty. Monkey fights never were.

"Ramok!" Mants ordered.

A muscle-bound pichu, who looked more like a howler, grabbed the most aggressive monkey by the neck. Ramok pulled him up and away with relative ease and plonked him down unceremoniously on the floor. Hormigas rushed in to restrain the other fighter, a rat-like monkey with a chunk missing from his left ear.

In the commotion, Claude seized his chance. He grabbed his notes, stowing them in his satchel, and slinked towards the reception, head down, as he aimed straight for the exit.

"Mr Talador," came a call, "leaving so soon?"

He stopped, turning to see the receptionist beckoning him over. "I've had word from the SI department that I'll be needed first thing."

"I see," said the wiry pichu. "How's your inspection gone, if you don't mind me asking?"

I do mind as it happens. Claude felt increasingly impatient in his desire to get out of the prison and into the open air. "Very impressive," he said. "Most impressive. Super organised. Well drilled. Great servants to the State."

"Why thank you, Mr Talador. And what of the staff?"

"I will mention Officer Mantel and you personally in my report. What was your name again?"

"Frederick Pimmler," he said, puffing out his ginger chest, unable to conceal a smile. "Do you need me to spell it? For your report."

"Sure. Pop it on the top here." Claude slammed the paper down.

"Of course," Pimmler said, clearly not reading the room and slowly scrawling his name in delicate tailwriting. "Thank you so much for coming. We're most humbled to have you."

"Yes, Frederick, it's been an honour for me too. A real eye opener."

"Always is—for you townies." Frederick smiled, his head twitching involuntarily. "All the best, Mr Talador. I'm eager to see the report. And I do hope we will be seeing you again sometime?"

"I look forward to it," said Claude, cursing under his breath as he was checked by the hormigas and allowed to pass out through the revolving door. He left without the inclination to say no such report would ever be in circulation. *Frederick Pimmler will never be an important monkey. Never.*

***

The early evening air brought relief, a freedom of sorts, but the first menacing call of the howlers shuddered through the trees; even this far out east they still assaulted the ears. He peered back round at the Pen, ensnared again by the unusual amount of colour. The old monkey was already back in his garden, pottering about. Claude knew he should leave.

Something drew him to the pocket of paradise instead. The gardener was digging away at a network of old roots, looking thoroughly content with the challenge of the task.

He looked up after a while. "Did she pass?"

"Pardon?" said Claude.

"Did she pass?" he repeated, passing over a shovel. "You're here on behalf of the Holy One, right?"

"My business is my own," said Claude, sinking the tool into the damp earth.

"She'll pass," the gardener said, turning back to his task. "Because she's the wrong target."

Claude cocked his head. "Excuse me?"

"All in good time." The gardener leant on his spade, his weathered hand brushing the ground, gathering up what looked like a pipe. "Name's Ludere, by the way." A smile flickered across his lips.

"I'm Claude."

Ludere prepared the pipe, arthritic fingers packing it with something from the garden. The scent of smouldering herbs infused the air. "Take a bit, Claude. All work, no play makes Jack a dull monkey."

Setting the shovel on the floor, Claude grasped the pipe, tracing the markings along its front, carvings depicting a fire weaving through the trees, watched over by two monkeys and a bird perched in the canopy. He brought it to his lips and inhaled, savouring the resinous flavour and warmth. A kind of punk for sure, yet sweeter. A fine batch, high-grade.

"They must pay you well here," said Claude.

"Not particularly." Then, with a conspiratorial look, Ludere whispered, "I grew this myself. One of the perks of being a seasoned gardener."

"I've clearly gone into the wrong profession." Claude passed back the pipe and felt for his badge.

"No choice is wrong in my mind," said Ludere. "You can always make another. Circumstances can change quickly, so keep your eyes open."

"Not forward?"

"That too." Ludere smiled, tending to the strange beak-like flower, even more stunning close up. It made Claude think of the recent night at the Agumon, the thick layer of mist and what he had seen fly through it …

"*Strelitzia reginae*," said Ludere, twirling it round without breaking the stem. "The bird of paradise flower. A perennial,

100

with beauty hard to match."

Claude did not disagree. "Not quite the real thing, though, is it?"

"Well, that depends on what you see. It's your reality." Ludere smiled again. "Do you believe in destiny, Inspector?"

"Nope."

"Well, if you could, you might see life a little differently …"

The two monkeys spoke for what seemed like days. Years even. Something of the East. Something of what lay beyond the mist. Something of the past, the times of Fuerza, Tiarra and the Hundred. A lot about the plants. A little about freedom, magic and songs.

When Claude finally set off west, he allowed himself one last glimpse back to the garden. The old pichu appeared to be talking to himself, patting thin air around his shoulder. Touching something …

Claude squinted, eyes drawn to the treeline beyond the garden. *Is that?*

He blinked. Still there.

The silhouette of a small bird perched among the branches. Watching Claude. A single eye, turned to face him, twinkling in the pale orange moonlight. *Strelitzia reginae?*

Chapter Ten

Refuge From The Darkness

Can you say for sure what you think is a dream is not actually reality? When you dream, it feels so real. When you wake, fragments of its memory linger. Life can feel like a dream. Going through the motions of the Commute and working life. A dull nightmare for some. Craving to return to the dream world. The question that always puzzles me concerns death. Is this when you come alive? Or do you enter a new dream?

- Mon Tiki -

Claude reached Hussleton just as the 8 p.m. whistle blast marked the official end of day, battling against the mass exodus of tired townies who jostled and barged their way home.

Only one monkey acknowledged his arrival on Floor 9. "Don't ask," he muttered before she could question him.

"You know I will," said Beena, who had clearly held on, hoping to catch her colleague. "I can stay a bit?"

"Don't be silly," said Claude, sighing as he fell into his chair. "Your family will be waiting. There's a nice moon tonight."

She gave Claude a hurried hug. "Sure you're okay? The Pen is not for the faint-hearted, I'm told."

"I've had better workdays." He shrugged, then fiddled around with the piles of paper on his desk, plucking out a small bag hidden in one document pack. Giving it a little wave. "But I've got this for when I'm done."

Beena shook her head. "I see your game, mister. Get in before the whistle, a bit of overtime, and earn yourself an extension on curfew."

"Something like that," said Claude. "Don't suppose Karo's still about?"

"He's back in. Very quiet though, very stressed. I do worry about him." They exchanged knowing nods. "There's something for you, by the way." She pointed towards the office cubbyholes.

"Excellent." Claude jumped from his seat, interest piqued. "Now you, get lost!"

"I'm going," she said, flinging her bag over her shoulder and flashing him a smile. "Oh, and I saved you a sugar lichen sandwich."

"Bye, gorgeous," Claude hollered when she reached the door, receiving scowls from the remaining late workers—Dubbert included.

Ignoring the stares, he picked up an official-looking envelope from the SI post, his name detailed in a strange scrawl. He bobbed his way back to his chair, the sound of the rain now hammering outside. One of the few perks of being a townie—sheltered well from the elements. Claude ripped open the seal and pulled out a tailwritten message.

> *Mr Talador,*
>
> *Hope your time 'inside' went well. After looking at things with a few of my Acolytes, we have decided to give Tom Huckbane an additional two percent for the work at the Dump. I wish we could do more, only it is not that straightforward. I am sure a seasoned business-monkey like Tom will understand. The denial of the extra funds is nothing to do with his work or yours. I am impressed with your first report. Glad to hear there were no signs of Monkey Business. I wait to receive your report on Officer Mantel.*
>
> *The fire of Fuerza be with you,*
> *Your Head of Department*

Claude let out a growl, scrunched up the note and chucked it in the direction of the nearest bin. It missed.

Dubbert chose that exact moment to shuffle over, leaning his head right into Claude's cubicle. "Not like you to stay—"

"Not now, Grouse," snapped Claude. "Get out of my space."

"You seem upset. Wanna talk?"

"With a hormiga like you? Certainly not."

"Why don't you ever work from your pod?" asked Dubbert.

A sharp snort escaped. "I can't think of anything more tragic."

"Tragic?" Dubbert scowled. "You might need to do it when that stack topples and you're stuck here past moonrise … don't say I didn't try to help."

Claude fired a threatening strike of his tail. *He's worse than the damn muddies.* Dubbert muttered as he pootled back to his own workstation. "I get twice as much done in half the time in my pod …" *And always has to have the last word.*

The luvé flickered, signalling the hour. Claude turned his attention back to the mess. The tasks did not seem to shrink, no matter how hard he stared. Bark scrolls hung off the edges, loose parchment threatened to scatter. The thought of cramming it all into his satchel and hauling it to the Dormor Tree did not fill him with joy.

Claude chuntered under his breath. "What did I really expect for Huckster? Extra State salt is hard to come by, he said. Unless it's for the new TVA expansion."

He looked up. Faint torchlight shimmered from Karo's office. Claude hastened over, passing Dubbert in the process; the turd-flinging monkey was studying a crumpled piece of paper. The one he had literally just thrown in the bin. Well, near the bin. Snatching it back, he growled. "You snake!"

"Good start that," said Dubbert, showing his teeth in a grin that was not remotely friendly. "Wasn't it your first inspection?"

"At least some of us get to go outside of Floor 9. Occasionally."

"I've got a bad back," said Dubbert. "You know that. And at

least some of us get to make it back for curfew. Occasionally."

"One moon, Grouse, I'll put you in the dirt. I promise you that." Claude fired another shot with his tail in Dubbert's direction, sending a pencil pot flying. Dubbert hissed a vicious form of goodbye, scrambling to pick the stationery up off the floor.

Claude laughed as he made his way over to the chink of light coming from underneath the door. The sign on the solid timber read: *Mr Shi – busy.*

Mr Shi did not respond to the first two knocks. Without trying a third, Claude barged in. Papers were strewn all over the place. In the corner, a half-eaten banana, now more mould than fruit, festered in its own demise. Two flickering candles were almost out of wick, casting a feeble, trembling light. A sorry-looking silver monstera drooped in a pot crusted with dried soil, withered leaves curling in defeat. None of these items masked the scent of dry sweat. And then there was Karo, slumped, head over a dusty desk, resting at an awkward angle.

Is the poor chap dead? Off to meet the Balban Reaper. Two in one day …

But no. A slow and steady yawn emanated from Karo's chubby chops. Then a loud snuffle before his head bobbed forward again. An even louder snore erupted from his nostrils.

"Oi, slob!" Claude's gruff voice reverberated around the room. "Sort yourself out."

He did not stir. Claude marched over, grabbed Karo's shoulder, and gave him a firm shake. The pichu awoke with a splutter. "Don't hurt me! I've done nothing wrong."

"That's debatable. What are you doing sleeping in this dive? Don't you spend enough time here?"

"Oh, oh! Sorry, chap," Karo spluttered, knuckling his eyes with stubby fingers. "I was having a bad dream. It was that night at the Drunken Monkey, the vampire bats were swirling, and that tall Acolyte—"

"Snap out of it," said Claude. "You're here now, in the safety of the office. Unless those candles burn down the whole joint."

"No, no, no." Karo was out of his seat, faffing with papers and jowl quivering. "I should be back at the Dormor Tree."

"Wait a moment, chap. Look what I've just received from the Head of Department."

"The Head of Department?" Karo stopped mid-faff. "Addressed directly to you?"

"Uh-huh, not good reading though," said Claude, passing it over.

His more senior colleague read the note, tail arcing up in concern. "The rotters! That's barely even inflation. I'm getting jolly fed up of this place."

So now you want to join the party. "I can tell." Claude looked round at the mess of an office. "Really not like you to fall asleep on the job though."

"I know," said Karo. "I'm up to my eyeballs in reports, not even had an evening to trim my nose hairs. Head of Department keeps asking for more details on treeper tax evasion. It's never simple. This role is decision after decision after decision."

"You're speaking to the Head of Department?"

"Well, through the hormigas, yes. One has taken to waiting outside my door. Checking to see why I might be … falling behind. They wanted to come and sit in with me the other day, but I told them to swivel."

Claude scoffed, leaning against the desk. "And that went down?"

"Badly. Very badly in fact. Two came in place of them today, and one said that a formal complaint had been made against me. 'Technical errors', they called it. Another mark on my record and I could be out with the treepers, sawing bark for a living. Imagine me, out there, trying to climb trees? I'd snap a branch on the way up. Although … at least I'd know how to fiddle some of the tax."

"You need to be careful," said Claude under his breath. "They'll get you if they can."

"Oh, don't worry about me, chap." Karo waved away the concern, demeanour shifting to exaggerated optimism. "I'll get on top of it. When I really think about it, I'm not in a bad position, am I? Not a million moons from State pension age. I'll get a nice chuck of aethersalt for retiring, then I'll have all the time in the world. Do what I want, spend more nights at the Cashew, join the jungle gym, sit in the chillauna. More quality time with Bo and the pichlets. You know, a proper family monkey at last."

Claude nodded. "I guess you're set." He did not look up, staring instead at the flickering candle. *What a life though. Is that my path too?*

"Won't be that long now," said Karo. "Anyway, where've you been today?"

"Our delightful Penitentiary. Not somewhere you'd want to end up in a hurry."

Karo frowned, disposed of the banana and patted him on the shoulder. "I know. Had an uncle down there once. Got beaten so bad he lost both eyes and half his tail. Never quite recovered. Later went mad and was packed into the Nuthouse, I think they called it."

"The Centre for Distressed Minds."

"That was it." Karo shivered. "Didn't go see him mind. They said he'd scare the pichlets, and me. Better left alone."

"To fester?"

Karo locked the door behind them, turning his sign round to *Out of Office*. He stopped. "Sad, really. He wasn't that bad a monkey. Only went in for dealing a bit of punk."

"A true criminal." *I should get a life sentence.* "Come on, chap, let's get out of here."

They departed Floor 9, vacant except for Dubbert, taking the lift in silence, both deep in thought. Claude did not get the usual kick passing out the turnstiles. A tropical shower had swept in also. He turned to Karo and pointed under the brow of a larger palm. "Sure you don't fancy a quick stop? Close out another truly shit day in the rainforest."

"Umm, I better not," said Karo, looking down the sodden path out of Hussleton. "Bo said to come straight home to groom her fur."

That monkey uses her whip more than the hormigas. And not in a good way! "Come on," Claude tried, grabbing his colleague by the shoulders. "One for good health. Wait out this storm."

Karo rolled his eyes. "One puff. That's all I'm having with you. Time doesn't grow on trees, chap."

***

Claude padded through the twilit forest towards Dormor 43. The storm had passed, replaced by a clearer night, where the Orange Moon shone like a beacon. The smoke with Karo had been short but sweet. Well, more short than sweet. His colleague had gone on a rant about how the Pen was all that stood between the Tribe and anarchy. A harsh place needed to deal with the necessary evil that would build up in society if left unchecked. Claude was not so sure. It had appeared that most of the inmates were in there for "political" crimes, petty felonies, or treepers on trumped-up charges. He could not get the image of the death row pichu out of his mind, kicking the damp leaves as he travelled. What had the monkey possibly done to deserve such a fate?

A sharp crack shot from the surrounding trees. Claude looked round, tail raised, poised for defence. Nothing except the shifting shadows. He hurried on. Then something snapped.

A branch? Off in the canopy. He stopped, not moving, breaths shallow, still seeing nothing more than a black wall of jungle. Another sound. A frog-like croak, not entirely of this world. He moved towards it instinctively, off the path, battling the sharper bits of undergrowth. Cobwebs attached themselves to his fur, and he shuddered as he swiped them from his face. It was a wilder, more primitive part of the rainforest, and his ears strained for another sound.

A reflection of light met his eyes.

An eye. A black pupil encased in a shining blue lid. An eye leading him away. Deeper into the twilight. He struggled to move silently, wary there could be hormigas about. Or worse.

The eye shut, and he lost his target.

He continued on, scrambling over fallen trunks and crumbling foliage until he reached an opening to a clearing where the moon cast an orange haze. The eye flashed again from the far end, and the frame of the watcher was revealed. A bird, the size of the one he had seen at the Agumon, with a large beak. The same form that Arabella had drawn in the Nest turned to its side and peered down at him, pupil glinting in the darkness.

"Who are you?" Claude spoke as loud as he dared.

The bird hopped back a few steps. It clicked its tongue and then bolted from the branch, shooting up into the dark abyss of the night.

"Wait!" Claude called out, moving fully into the clearing. With eyes only for the sky, he tumbled over a slippery rock-like object and fell to the ground. He scrambled in the direction of the tree where the bird had been. Fought his way through thick ancient roots, threaded his way through the network of creeping vines. Once at a tree trunk, he assessed the area; he was quite lost. It felt different to most of Tierra Libre—untouched moss and spiderwebs covered the trees. The usual chatter of the deathwatch cicadas stark in their absence. Almost tripping again, his foot collided with something, causing a loud crunch that pierced the night. A curse escaped Claude's lips. Digging through the tangle of leaves, his fingers blindly probed until they closed around an object. He brought it closer, raising it to eye level. Empty sockets stared back. His grip slackened, and *the thing* tumbled to the floor.

A monkey skull. Strewn about the base of the tree were scattered remnants. He crouched, catching his breath, studying the objects closer up. Bones of long-deceased pichus? Fragments of skeletons? One of the old death camps? Stories, and souls, erased from history. *As if this day couldn't get any darker.*

Claude's gaze darted between the path he had just followed and the unexplored trail ahead. Fear whispered, urging him to turn back. This was risky business.

Yet, nagging inquisitiveness won. He moved forward. In the distance, he thought he could make out a faint light. Flickering. *A torch, maybe?*

"Who goes there?" came a sharp shout.

Shit! Claude dived behind a tree, staying as still as possible, hand over his mouth.

"I've seen you." The voice spoke again. A male voice. Challenging.

He crouched down further, preparing to crawl his way out using the roots as cover. There was still a chance to slip away into the night.

"Reveal yourself, pichu!" More forceful this time.

Claude peeked round the tree, the darkness now illuminated by a small flame, a torch fashioned from timber. It revealed the frame of a tall monkey. A hood of dark leaves shrouded his face. He headed straight for Claude at a cautious pace. Eyes darting from side to side.

Maybe the pichu is bluffing? Maybe he hasn't seen me? What's he guarding?

A muddie buzzed near Claude's face. He swatted it. A whoosh of air. The monkey's gaze turned right back to the tree. He continued his approach. Only a pichuleap away, he halted, sniffing the air in the manner of a focused hunter.

Claude acted on an impulse he could not quite define. There was no doubt. He took a slow breath, then stepped out into the torchlight. Raising his hands and tail, putting himself in fate's path.

"My, my, my," exclaimed the monkey. "What brings you to these parts so late at night?"

"I must have lost my way," said Claude. "Tough day at the office, if you know what I mean?"

"I know exactly what you mean," replied the hooded stranger. "I hope all is well with the Holy One?"

"She's well, as far as I can tell," said Claude, puzzled by the accent, among many other things.

The stranger looked up to the moon, then chuckled. "So, why are you *really* here, Claude Talador?"

Claude almost choked in response. "How do you know my name?"

"I know a lot about this rainforest," said the monkey, enjoying this thoroughly it appeared. "I often keep my real face masked, my voice too. My eyes though, are always open."

"Well, that's lovely for you," said Claude. "Must be on my way. Good evening to you." He pivoted away from the figure, darting back towards the clearing.

"Wait. Do you not want to know why a pichu is out here so late at night?" The monkey spoke to Claude's tail.

Claude stopped still. Curiosity was not a sin. He twisted, facing the hooded figure once more. The eyes had a hint of kindness in them, not threatening, despite their determination. *Familiar somehow* …

"So what is a pichu like you doing out this late at night?"

"I can only show you," he said. "You must see to believe."

"My eyes are open too," said Claude. "Although it's pretty dark right now."

"Ahh, if only there were more like you. An open monkeymind is a rare trait these days." The stranger paused. Within striking distance, surely. Claude did not back away. Nor did he attack.

"Before I show you, I must get one thing straight." The monkey looked around the jungle before turning back to Claude. "I am a monkey of my word. I trust you are too?"

"You can trust me."

"Yes, I do believe that." The monkey eyed him cautiously now. "Although there's more at stake than my own fur. I must ask you keep secret all that is to come." He pointed the flame back. "If you do that, I can help you. If you can't do that, well, now is the time to turn back. As if this meeting never happened. Nothing lost, nothing—"

"I won't say a word."

"I trust that too, Inspector." The monkey slowly peeled back his hood and mask.

"No way!" Claude blinked and shook his head. "You snake, that accent—"

"Was completely necessary," said Tom Huckbane. "One cannot be too careful outside of curfew. I'm sure you agree?"

"Yes," said Claude, breaking into a relieved smile. His turn to pause. "I must apologise first. The Head of Department just got back to me. It's not good news."

"I've already heard. On the jungle drums."

"You have? Two percent is a joke."

"And not a hugely funny one." Huckster sighed. "But not unexpected. The State doesn't show support for business-monkeys like me. If I'm honest, I think they'd rather take the Dump back under their control. Except they can't bear the stench." He flashed a wry grin. "Or the margins. Anyway, tonight is not a night for politics. So, now, will you tell me what brought you here?" As he spoke, the moon appeared to rise ethereally behind him.

"I was following something," said Claude, thinking of the bird.

"That makes sense," said Huckster. "I guess we all are in a way."

Holding his torch aloft, Huckster gestured to Claude to follow. He led them away from the lookout tree. The light of the flame and glow of the moon allowed a clear view of a pathway through the undergrowth. Huckster whispered as they went, moving quickly. "It's been a long time in the making this place. A cocoon of safety from those in power. A new world ..."

They scaled a fallen giant of a tree. Roots twisted, reaching skywards. Huckster paused. "Come on, my friend. The Refuge of Learning awaits."

***

The entrance was easy to miss, concealed by a mass of dense foliage, no X marking the spot. Huckster showed the way, removing a latticework contraption that gave way to a circular opening in the ground. He commenced an ungainly descent, crawling through the small tunnel. Claude dragged himself along behind, feeling a few slimy worms, and probably worse, wriggling in his fur. As they went lower underground, the air became sticky. Claustrophobia coiled round him like a stranglehold. He had never ventured beneath the soil before—the world above ground had always been his playground.

After a few minutes of scrabbling, they were able to rise, emerging into a cavern. It appeared to have been dug out over decades, with great timber pillars supporting the ground above. No other monkeys were present here, although a voice murmured from further away. Claude strained to hear it. He could also almost taste incense now—smoky sandalwood and berry scents filled the air. Huckster signalled his follower through another hollow chamber.

They reached a larger hall; an ornate table in its centre held a luvé lamp and what looked like ancient scrolls. The air seemed cooler down here; a row of dusty bookcases lined one side. Claude headed towards the old tomes, appreciating the neat and alphabetised ordering. He travelled to the far end of the hall and looked up. A banner with faded lettering hinted the Refuge had been around for a while. The words still legible.

Ignorance is bliss, ignorance is danger.
Comfort is convenient, comfort is danger.
Acquiescence is safe, acquiescence is danger.

A hand gripped his shoulder. Huckster was by his side. "Put this on." He handed over a mask. "It'd be best to conceal your identity at this stage."

"Sure," said Claude, taking hold of it. There were slits for his eyes and ears, a tapered string to the back. He put it on, fingers shaking ever so slightly.

This room with the books and banner was not even the end of the underground lair. It was an entrance to another room. The sound of a voice clearer now. Huckster put a finger to his lips. His other hand reached for the handle of a set of sliding doors. He opened them without a sound.

"Well, I'll be damned," murmured Claude.

Joan, the monkey from the night of the Blood Red Moon, commanded centre stage in a vast cave. A group of bowed monkeys hung on her every word as she addressed them. She spoke of pichus sleepclimbing through life. Going through the motions. Watching the moons pass by. Her words resonated, stirring a sense of awakening within. He took a pew near the back. There was something about her voice. Sage, absorbing.

"One can notice an emergent distrust in the very institution supposed to protect us," she said. "The State was set up for the Tribe. But the State has lost sight of the best interests of its Tribe members."

Claude could not take his eyes off the monkey. Her specks of green glistened in the low light. Every word beckoned him to listen more intently.

"A select few are starting to pull the vines from their eyes. Trusting what they see, not only what they hear. Thinking beyond what they are told. We must keep our minds open. Seek solace in these monkeys who look for truth."

The breath he had been holding slipped out; the incense was even stronger now. *Have I stumbled into a dream?*

"Lowering the volume of the State can feel as hard as felling a banyan tree with your own tail. We come to believe the stories we are brought up with, the memes that are repeated, becoming victims of our programming. Anyone saying different is judged to commit the high crime of Monkey Business and viewed akin to a bald monkey peddling fur growth powder." She stopped there, allowing a few laughs from the front to fizzle out. "Most pichus take the path of least resistance. Bury their thoughts of something more, thoughts of change. They suppress the songs of the heart. Look upon the TVA with fear. You must understand this … the feelings of discontent are real. These rules of life decreed, they are the illusion."

"What can we do?" asked a voice near the stage. "Our numbers are so small."

"One cannot simply creep up to the Monvida and end the oppression," she replied. "Careful, quiet resistance is the way forward. Sometimes you must start singing on your own before others take up the song too. A moon will come when natural harmony is restored to our trees. When pichus can climb freely again, treepers and townies alike. Take strength from this sanctuary. The State can only take away freedom in the external world, not what lies inside. May the light of Tiarra shine with you."

"And on you, Joan Saei," the audience replied together.

She closed her eyes and seemed to be murmuring something to herself, then out to them. An incantation. A long silence followed. He took it all in. Studying the others present. Half bowed their heads as if in prayer. The others looked forward. Inquisitive eyes flashing in the firelight.

A large smile formed on Claude's lips. A smile that even his new mask could not hide.

These were his monkeys.

Chapter Eleven

Growing Underground

The thriving moons of the Tribe must not be lost forever. A time will come when one can recapture the essence of the source. Channel it into a new dawn. Look for the arrival of the Emeral. An unconflicted spirit. A new vision. The bringer of balance to the forest.

- Nyx Sylva -

The Refuge of Learning quickly became Claude's favourite place in Tierra Libre. Not that this was difficult. Two whole moons had passed, with as many evening trips as he could manage. In that time, he had grown closer to Joan Saei. The wise, albeit surreptitious soul had seen through his mask straight away. She had also taken on responsibility for initiating him into the group. Looking after his development with unexplained dedication. Her instructions were deliberate, her words often mysterious but laced with a confidence that demanded trust. Training occurred in various forms—the art of mind-less-ness, reading signs of the forest, holons, lucid dreaming, moon charts, and the prestigious art of swordplay.

The pair duelled with blunted timber blades in their tail tips under the watch of flickering firelight. The clash of wood echoed, vibrations coursing through him with every strike. The cool air of the underground lair created the ambience of a dojo from times of old.

Beads of sweat ran down his face, matting his fur as he raised his blade once more.

"Trust your instincts," said Joan, sending a few sword thrusts his way. He backed each attack off with a grimace. Countered with an upward swing. But her defence was swift. Almost effortless in execution. Pain shot through all his nerve endings as Joan blocked a low swipe. His footing faltered. Positioning all wrong. The weight of her next strike sent him toppling backwards, flying over a table. A mass of books tumbled down from above, burying him.

"We're not done," she said, hauling him up and out.

He stretched out his joints, the ache reminding him of his earlier failure, regained his blade, and turned to face her again. "This time is mine."

"You said that last time." She smiled, sending her sword straight for his chest.

He twisted out of the way. Rolled to her side. Swinging at her legs.

She blocked again and leapt back. Snarling. The older pichu had the skill and nous. Claude had the speed, agility and boldness to at least give her a good fight. So he thought anyway, fighting on.

"You grow stronger," she said, sending a controlled volley of blows back at her opponent.

"Come off it!" said Claude, gasping for breath as he repelled them. "I haven't won a single bout."

His energy was already fading. But he could not let that show. Tightening his grip, he tested a few powerful attacks of his own, focusing with everything he had. Again, she repelled with seeming ease. Her breathing was heavier now though. The rise and fall of her chest a fraction faster. He had a chance.

Joan pounced again. A well-placed jab almost pierced the skin of his torso that would have signalled the familiar end. Only he managed a desperate swipe to save that skin. Knocking her back. She steadied herself instantly, let out a chuckle.

She came at him with an arcing crosscut that Claude was unable to block. He lost his balance, crashing into another bookcase. More books tumbled down. As he lay under the pile of ancient tomes, she put a foot on his blade, her own sword to the nape of his neck. He yielded.

"Your time will come," she said, resting her blade on her shoulder. Not helping him up this time. "You're certainly improving; that was our longest duel yet. Your skills are developing fast."

"So you say." Claude sighed, hauling himself up and flopping into the nearest chair.

She chucked a dusty book onto his lap. "Now for the important stuff."

Claude glanced at the fire-charred copy of *The Seven Core*

Teachings of Tiarra. "I've read this cover to cover already," he said, flipping the book open to its familiar pages and letting it fall shut again. "Twice."

"Patience," she said, as if the word alone were answer enough.

"Patience." He rolled his eyes, slumping further into the chair. This was even harder than the work with the blade. "A virtue easier to preach than practise."

"Practise it, you must." She gestured towards the text as she made to leave him alone in the old library. "Start from page one. See what you missed."

***

The armchair beside the books provided a wonderful hideout filled with quiet. Claude caught the faint scent of smoke as he read Tiarra's fifth teaching: *Working for a Living.* The lesson unfolded like a conversation through time, sparking insights on the merits of a different way. Each turn of the page pulled him deeper into the ageless wisdom, speaking to the doubts that lingered, *mostly* unspoken, in his mind.

Was working to live really a fact of life? Or was it an invention of those in power, fed to the open minds of monkeys in the newly formed Tribe? Tiarra posed how "work" was installed as the ultimate virtue for an individual to prove their worth. It was not nature, the text argued—it was nurture. A system imposed to quiet dissent, to ensure that obedience would become the unquestioned norm.

Claude leant back, staring at the ceiling. He agreed. The ethics of Fuerza, the God of Work—strength and stoicism—had been co-opted by the State. A fine line between fulfilment and exploitation. Had that line been crossed? Yes, hard work was essential, but not at the cost of all else.

Tiarra had written suggestions for a more balanced approach. But whole phrases were indecipherable, the text no longer legible. Specks of worn ash clung stubbornly to the pages, obscuring passages. He brushed off what he could, careful not to damage what remained, bringing the book closer to his face, adjusting it to catch the light.

It reminded him of something Sura had told him—the tale of how all fiction stories and rebellious texts had been smuggled away before the book burnings. How some truly learned souls had braved flames and rescued books mid-blaze. Reading each text, therefore, was a blessing, an almost sacred act. A challenge too. A challenge that rewarded its reader with complex ideology and hidden meanings. Inspired, Claude delved into a variety of topics from history to anarchy to practical philosophy, devouring them all like a famished howler before breakfast.

"I should've had you down as a bookworm that day you came to the Dump," said Huckster, pulling up a chair beside him. A mischievous twinkle danced in his brown eyes. "You still interested in that book of mine?"

Claude paused, folded his page and placed the book on the floor. He eyed the monkey beside him. "Why would I need that now? I've got all these." He pointed in the direction of the bookcases, shelves bowing under the collective weight of untapped wisdom.

Huckster grinned. "Ah, these shelves may hold a multitude of knowledge, but this is something special. A map to break free from the chains of conformity."

"Tell me more."

"Imagine, my friend, a world where the song in your heart is not silenced but amplified, where pichus rise above the constraints imposed by the Monkey State." As Huckster spoke, he revealed he had brought the book with him, clutching it to his chest like a proud infant showing off their most prized possession. "This book," he said, holding it just out of Claude's reach, "holds the key to freedom."

Claude's heart quickened. His hand reached out without his permission; he snatched it away. "An interesting offer. Who's it by again?"

"J. Semmelwise Locke," whispered Huckster, leaning in. "A true renegade."

"Not a famous monkey," Claude replied, itching his chin. "Are they still alive?"

"I wouldn't know … But, the author certainly claims to know what lies beyond the mist. Is that something you can say for anything on Ms Saei's syllabus?"

He's got me there. "Five grams of aethersalt."

Huckster shook his head, clicking his tongue. "At least eight."

"I could stretch to six."

"Seven and you have a deal."

"Done."

"I think it'll be right up your tree," said Huckster, passing it over and shaking Claude's tail.

Claude tucked it into his satchel. "I'll sneak it home after the lecture tonight."

***

The hidden underground sanctuary came alive during the lectures. Meetings were usually held very late in the evening, once a week, and pichus slinked in, wearing their masks. The talks shared a common theme, speaking of what Claude had felt to be true in his gut, now laid before his eyes.

One of the main lecturers, Maude Leaper, an athletic-looking monkey, chose not to shield her identity. Though Claude was not convinced that was her real name. And he was certainly not convinced she was a normal monkey. To risk such candid discussions must have put her life in danger.

As Maude spoke, small stakes of fire crackled on either side of her. Shrouding her face in a mystical light. An interplay of light and dark.

"Our current system has been effective," she concluded, "but the cost is becoming too great. We will have to be the catalysts. To open others' eyes and bring luvé back to the rainforest."

The sanctuary erupted in a roar from the Refugers. A standing ovation followed. Claude felt his fur stand on end. Igniting something deep within.

The fire lingered long after the lectures ended. His nights became the time he was really awake—passionate and alive. His days, by contrast, were becoming as dull as the views in Hussleton. He still buried himself in the idle goings on of Floor 9. His conversations with Karo had taken on a painful irony. Small talk felt shallow. Beena seemed to sense something was up, but he was comfortable swatting her prying questions away as he would a persistent muddie. And then there was Dubbert, who seemed to pester him more than usual, growing more irksome with each passing day. Claude had taken to whipping him viciously with his tail whenever he ventured too close—that seemed to do the trick.

Claude found himself caring less and less for the new SI assignments—the Putrid Pond, the Timber Processing Yard, and the Nut Counting Facility. Tasks handled with detached efficiency.

He had only spotted one townie, an impetuous youth from Floor 4 who called himself Trent. They would nod to each other if ever their paths crossed above ground. Nothing more. Discretion was urged by the leaders of the Refuge. But secrets always carried danger; Claude knew that much.

It was not that far from dawn now, the darkness not so deep, as he moved through the rainforest. He squinted up at Dormor 43. Readying himself to climb without a sound. Even the ever-suspicious Grouse had abandoned his neighbourhood watch, lulled by the late hour. Claude's ploy had been simple: check into the Dormor Tree early in the evening, ideally with a nod to his crusty colleague, then slip out later, unnoticed, climbing down the back of the tree once the night had deepened.

He clambered upwards, aided by lianas—thick, interwoven vines that twisted their way up the trees in search of light. Claude crept inside his pod, closing the door and hoping it would not squeak, letting out a deep breath once back within its confines. A safety of sorts. He glugged down a cup of water and lit the candles on either side of his bed before collapsing onto its hard frame. For a moment, he simply lay there, letting his breathing slow. But sleep would not come swiftly, events of the night refusing to settle. The energy of the lecture, Maude's words, the roar of the crowd …

With a groan, he sat up and reached for his satchel. Retrieved his new possession. He propped himself up against the wall and opened the book to the introduction.

> *You may not believe what you are about to discover. A challenging puzzle for even the craftiest monkeymind. You may dismiss almost all you read in these coming pages. A series of riddles. A consolidation of ideas. One defining solution. And yet—if you can suspend disbelief until the conclusion—you may well be rewarded with a treasure that is beyond all measure …*

Chapter Twelve

Proper Education

The youth are the only ones truly free—until they learn to see.

- Huì Sarr -

"**G**et your badge," Tia barked. "You're a wanted monkey." Her sharp tone cut through Claude's buzzing mind. As the rainforest commenced its slow cooking for the day ahead, he skulked his way round the familiar circular Commute.

She was watching him, waving him to the side. *Shit! Something's up.*

"For what?" he said, shoulders tensing. *She can't know. They would've come straight to my pod.*

"Monkey Business, of the highest order." She pointed away from the main clearing. "Move. Quickly."

Claude followed. An awkward obedience. His eyes darted side to side; a few other monkeys watched on under their noses.

Should I flee? But where? The Agumon? Out East? Into the trees?

Out of view of all the other monkeys, Tia turned and faced him. A smile like the Monvida's.

I was wrong to dismiss Grouse. The snake has slithered. He must've spotted me. Ignorance is danger! It's written at the Refuge after all.

"You look like you've seen a borderbeing," said Tia. "You getting any sleep?"

"Loads," he muttered, trailing behind her, still searching the surrounding rainforest for an escape.

"Cut the howler crap." She stopped, moved closer. Pulled his chin up. "You look awful."

He pinched her on the nose, making her jerk backwards. "Look who's talking."

"Petty," she said, swatting him with her tail. "Anyway, we need to talk."

I could still make it to the trees. As far as I can climb. Never be seen again …

"I bring word of your next inspection."

"Oh, right." The weight of a howler dropped off his back. "Where will that be?"

"She asked me to relay her orders directly. The Holy One wants you down south. Pack an overnight bag—you'll be going back to school. There are two teachers to keep an eye on. Rumours of divergence from the curriculum, pupils being let off class early, signs of Monkey Business. This obviously must be nipped in the bud." Tia winked. "Of course, we could get the hormigas to do all that. But what we really need to discover is *why*. Why it's happening. Teachers are a key cog of society, and deviance from youngsters is unheard of, rare in the extreme. Yet, its threat is insidious. Like a virus. Unless contained early, of course.

Eradicated. At source."

Tia looked away from him then, shaking her head. "She also said to mention that you've been selected for your intelligence. And discretion."

Claude smirked. "At least someone appreciates talent."

"We'll see about that," said Tia. "Just don't let us down."

"Us?"

"You'll also have an Acolyte with you ... covertly. Be nice to them. Be civil. I think those were her exact words." Tia, arms folded, now had a smirk across her own chops. "Quite the assignment, hey? She must see something in you after all. Either that or she doesn't trust your tail as far as she could swing it."

"It'll be a learning experience, I'm sure."

"Good from you," said Tia. "The prospect of more financial support should give the teachers a timely reminder of whom they serve. What can be gained by following the mandate of the State."

"Sure thing," he said. "So, who's this Acolyte I must be nice to? Don't tell me it's your sycophantic arse?"

"Ahh, the supposed intelligence rears its head before we've even got started. Yes, I'll be the one watching you, brother. Closely. Now, Eyes Forward, be a good monkey."

"Don't push your luck," said Claude, baring his teeth. *The Refuge is safe. That's all that matters.*

After a quick pit stop at Dormor 43, the Talador siblings set off again in heavy silence, neither inclined towards morning pleasantries. Claude lagged behind, clutching the small of his back and letting out an exaggerated groan.

"Ah, I must've twisted something back there," he muttered, wincing as he bent slightly at the waist.

Tia stopped and turned, narrowing her eyes. "Seriously? You were fine five minutes ago."

Oh, this is too easy. He took a dramatic step forward, dragging one foot behind, hand still pressed to his back.

Tia folded her arms. "You're unbelievable."

Claude flashed her a grin—slow and smug—the kind that had earnt him a few clipped ears as a youngster. He hobbled a little slower, teasing for a reaction ...

And there it was—a flicker of annoyance. The faintest clench of her jaw. Perfect. He let out another dramatic groan, biting back the urge to laugh. Her sharp inhale told him she was on the brink. But winding Tia up? Worth it every time.

Upon their arrival, Tia immediately sought a private meeting with the headmaster, leaving Claude free to roam the school trees, albeit with an efficient hormiga for company. It did not take long to see that pichu boarding school was no leisurely swing through the canopy these days, with lessons from 6 a.m. to 8 p.m., every single hour accounted for. The curriculum covered all the areas of being a "good young monkey". A large blackboard outlined a simple, stifling set of rules:

1. No Monkey Business

2. Eyes Forward

3. Always listen to and obey the staff

4. No playing or daydreaming during school hours

5. No climbing (except on the Tree of Growth)

6. No singing within the school canopy

7. No reading unauthorised books

8. Logic trumps intuition

9. It will be worth it in the end

10. No Monkey Business

Claude tried not to laugh. It was absurd, criminal even. *Pichlets aren't this stupid, surely?* Shaking his head, he eagerly scanned the compound, hoping to rediscover the landmarks of his own school days: the old jungle gym, the acrobat arena, his beloved nutball court. But as he explored, a sinking feeling settled within. He traced the paths, once alive with laughter, now eerily subdued. His fingers twitched, yearning to feel the exhilaration of the zip lines once more. But the zip lines were gone. The classrooms now stood as dull, symmetrical structures connected by a central corridor. Above, a roof of tightly laced vines hung stretched like a canopy, casting mottled shadows. The energy he remembered, the pulse of the place, had vanished—replaced by something rigid, restrained and hollow.

"Things have changed," he muttered under his breath.

"Yes," said the hormiga as they moved to the outer perimeter.

"The Holy One wanted things to become more regimented. More active control of the students' timetable, increasing the lesson time. More time for learning."

Claude sniggered, noticing the old kissing tree laden with graffiti—initials, declarations of young love and various attempted depictions of wild animals. "What about playtime?"

The hormiga raised an eyebrow. "Climbing practice was scrapped. Breaktime was years ago, Mr Talador. Focus now is on more productive pursuits."

They arrived at an enormous banyan tree. Thick, raking branches and numerous levels that stretched outwards and upwards. Once, it had been the centrepiece of the playground, where the students had used ropes to climb, dangle and frolic to their heart's content. He had spent countless hours here, laughing with friends—or wincing from a bruise courtesy of Tia and her cronies. He had loved this tree, though, an artefact of the rainforest. However, the banyan had clearly been converted for more practical purposes these moons. The ropes gone. The graffiti scrubbed off. Every trace of joy and chaos erased. Replaced by numbers on placards. Utilitarian script.

"The Holy One renamed this the Tree of Growth," said the hormiga. "It's quite the invention, really. As you'll see, each level has a number on it. Starting from one hundred right here. Students must work their way patiently up the tree. After one hundred moons, there's the graduation test to determine if they are ready to move into the adult world."

"Graduation to the adult world, is that how you frame it?"

"Well, yes," said the hormiga. "It marks the evolution a pichlet goes through in their time here. Gives them a constant target to strive for. A comprehensive incubation period, as the Monvida likes to call it."

"I see. Mind if I take a look?"

"Of course not. I'll wait here. I have no interest in climbing."

"Won't be a minute." Springing up the branches, Claude scaled his way to the number one spot, the muscle memory kicking in, along with the memories of the mind. He paused at the top, laughing at the absurdity of it all. The students tucked away in lessons; it was so quiet you could hear a brazil nut drop. A hormiga was perched in a distant surveillance tree. *What are they keeping guard over? These are pichlets, not revolutionaries.* Hopefully they would not spot him slinking out that evening.

"Are you nearly done, Mr Talador?" called the hormiga from below. "This feels like Monkey Business."

Claude zipped his way down. "All done," he said, barrel-rolling and springing to his feet.

Their route back to the main corridor took them past several lessons in full flow. The philosophy classroom door flew open.

"You can't tell me what to do!" screeched a little sprog of a pichlet as he was carried out. Two hormiga learning assistants pulled back the little one's arms as he writhed and wrestled, but to no avail.

"We can," said one hormiga.

"And we will," said the other.

"Okay, okay!" said the pichlet.

They let him go. He huffed and brushed down his fur, then turned his head to Claude. "What you looking at?" he sniped in vaguely intelligible Pichu.

Claude laughed. *Was I any different at his age?* And before he could reply, the assistants hauled the student off down the corridor. The struggle resuming.

"I'm sorry about that," said the hormiga. "Lot of energy, these youngsters. We can harness that. Not the worst thing in the world. That one will be in detention for a while now though."

"I assumed so," said Claude. "And that entails what exactly?"

"Oh, it's quite tame really," continued the hormiga. "They must hang backwards from a tree by their tail for up to an hour at a time. Not allowed to talk. With a healthy amount of time to think about what they've done wrong. At the end, they must apologise for their 'mistake' and vow to work harder in future. And write at least one hundred lines of—"

"No Monkey Business?"

The hormiga seemed to sneer back. "One learns through repetition, Mr Talador. It's the only way. It's a proper education here."

***

Claude sat twiddling his thumbs in the empty front row of a dingy room with nothing adorning the walls. A rumble of chairs came from behind him. Along with jabbering voices.

"Constant progress keeps the Tribe strong," announced a

doddery professor, entering at no great pace.

Mr Musk was his name for obvious, but unfortunate, reasons. *Things haven't improved. He smells worse than a hot, frothing pile of howler dung. This must be why they all crowd towards the back.* If truth be told, Claude was shocked to see the old codger still clinging on. *Still getting paid good salt, no doubt.*

"Economics is a study of precision," said Mr Musk. "Facts and figures. This is not a place for creative ideas." The teacher rocked about on his feet. "Thanks to intelligent leadership, we remain blessed with abundant resources. The rainforest rewards us for our initiative. Growth is good for everyone. Our great ancestors picked this canopy carefully. The world of infinite trees they called it." A gob ball of spit flew as Mr Musk got impassioned on his subject.

No, this is why they sit closer to the back!

"However, as you all should know by now, no economy can stand still. Progress must continue. This does mean we have to be more ruthless with our natural resources than those treeper huggers would advocate. Remember that one good tree, well taken care of, can fuel a family for a moon. However, for every two trees felled, at least one more should be planted—"

It should be one for one. Father would have his tail in a right old twist.

"—infinite supply is not possible, so an element of pragmatism is required. The Holy One is a staunch defender of economic theory." Musky started spluttering. Unable to stop. Cheeks turning bright red.

Claude nudged a cup of water in front of him. *Might be better if he choked and had done with it.* The teacher took it down in a single swig, then turned his back on the class.

"Umm, where was I?" Mr Musk said, turning to look directly at Claude. "I, err, encourage you all to view the world with logical eyes. Always question what value you can get from the things around you. A tree for shelter. Nuts for nutrition. Plants for pharmaceuticals. The rainforest provides in ample measure. But we must think of ways to get more from it. Now, I'd like to turn your attention to the handout. Please take the rest of the lesson to read it through and complete the questions within." Musky coughed once more. A few bits of saliva hit Claude's cheek. He wiped it off with his forearm. *I'm not paid nearly enough for this.*

"Oh," Musky finished, "need I mention rules one and three."

"Yes, sir," replied the class in a dull tone.

"Sorry, fellow"—he addressed Claude—"I get a bit excited when there are inspections. What's your name?"

"Claude Talador."

"Great, Mr Tador," said Musky, shuffling. "I know how important economics is to the Holy One. Do you have any questions for me?"

"It's Talador," said Claude without thinking it was worth the bother.

"I beg your pardon. Good with numbers, not with names. I do apologise."

"It's fine. So, if I understand it right, the main theme is

progress ... but sustainable. Why did you say there is no place for creative ideas?"

"Well, I can only speak for economics," said the professor, "but it's clearly specified in the syllabus that we should be wary of such a trait. We are the teachers. They are the followers. The use of imagination is considered unhealthy in a pichlet. Dreams are danger. Or something like that. The focus should be on the practicalities of life. I can't remember the exact wording. I do apologise, Mr Tador."

Not again.

"Talador," corrected Musky. "Sorry!"

The class chuckled behind Claude, clearly not as focused on their handouts as they were meant to be.

"No Monkey Business," blurted Musky, sending another spitball across the classroom. Claude was too quick this time, moving his head out of the line of fire. It landed on a nerdy-looking kid in the row behind.

"Ha!" Claude could not contain his amusement.

Hysterical giggles erupted.

"Quiet." Musky directed the pichlets again. "You're not a bunch of borderbeings ... Ahh, well, they're a young group, as you can tell. Haven't quite grasped the importance of economic theory and how it can lead to personal and combined prosperity just yet."

Musky was met by mute expressions, and the students seemed to decide to return to their work. Clearly better than listening to another Musky ramble; some things never change. What was more of a conundrum was why Tia and the Holy One were interested in this teacher. There was more chance of deviance from a hormiga.

"No problem, Professor," said Claude. "There's plenty of time for these young minds. Don't worry, I'm not here to analyse the application of the syllabus. You'll know that much better than me. I'll leave you and the students to get on."

"Oh yes, if you must, Mr Tador. Many thanks for coming today. Would you like one of the pichlets to show you out?"

"No, I'll be fine." Claude turned to exit the exceedingly stuffy classroom. He wondered if any of the students would make eye contact, but they all bowed their heads. Not one dared a glimpse up. *There's no virus here. They fear the State badge, no doubt, and what it means to their conditioned minds. I pity them. Pity for the heavily controlled future that's already upon them.*

Claude faffed around, looking busy, until the 8 p.m. whistle when a dutiful hormiga showed him to his lodgings for the evening. An exquisite room in the trees, to be fair. A double bed with a flexible wooden frame and a pleasant view of the canopy, looking away from the school. The State had spared no salt. Claude sat with a bosky, looking out as night drew in, misty rain playing against the backdrop of the Yellow Moon. *A taste of the High Life*, he mused, nibbling the delicious macadamias provided.

***

Claude sneaked his way spider-like down from the private dorm.

On the canopy floor, the thickness of the surrounding trees blocked out the moon and horizon. A closeness to the air, an eerie silence. He was almost out of the school grounds when he caught his leg on an acacia thorn.

"For Fuerza's sake!" he cursed, stooping down to pull it out, rubbing his shin. The chances of finding an aloe to soothe it were slim to none. Still he searched the soggy ground for something.

"Oi!"

Claude spun round like a guilty infant.

Tia shuffled towards him. "Where you shooting off to?" she asked, expression unreadable.

"None of your business."

"No, really? It's not long till curfew."

She's worse than Grouse. Will she plague me all my moons? "Thought I'd hit the jungle gym. Work on my leap."

She cocked her head. "Bit keen for a school night?"

"Every evening's a school night. After *Your Holiness* brought that latest law in."

"She's your Holy One too."

He thought he could sense ferment on her breath. Claude sniffed the air loudly. "What are you doing out, sister? As you say, it's almost curfew."

"State business." She looked towards the school rather than at Claude. The cogs in her brain clearly turning. "Private business."

"Naturally."

She paused, wiping her lip. "I may stop for a grub burger and chips at the Forager too."

"Haven't you already eaten?"

"Yeah, but they're so good. How are your lodgings anyway? She's been most kind, I trust?"

"Comfortable enough," said Claude, impatience bubbling. He had wanted to reach the Refuge early tonight. Huckster had called a special meeting. "They're spacious, well kept. And possess a delightful view of all this … err … rain."

"You can't do anything about the weather," said Tia, tutting. "Let's schedule a proper check-in. Tomorrow after school. We can go through the copious notes I'm sure you've collected on our targets. See what you think needs to be done."

"I can hardly wait."

"I bet," she said without a smile. "Enjoy your workout, brother."

"You should join?" he dared, knowing the answer.

"Oh no," she said, straightening her fur. "I leave that sort of thing to those of—lesser—intelligence."

"As you please." Claude dipped his head. "Catch you tomorrow."

Departing the school grounds, he sensed her eyes latch claw-like onto his back. Following him closely. Tracking him all the way into the night.

Chapter Thirteen

Leaps Of Faith

Freedom of body. Freedom of mind. They have similarities,
yes, but a key difference, no? You can break a monkey out of
prison, yet to help them more profoundly, you must point them
towards freedom of thought. The true means to break out.
Into a world completely their own.

—From "The Means to Escape" by Kien Tol

Claude travelled swiftly under the gaze of the glistening Yellow Moon; the steady patter of rain kept the cicadas quiet. He knew the path like a howler knows dawn, doubling back around near the jungle gym. Tia could have eyes in other trees. She was a suspicious soul at the best of times. He pushed her out of his monkeymind. It stirred his heart to leave the real world for a short while, finding his way through the old cemetery as quickly and quietly as possible, only his mask and dreams for company.

Tonight, his heart was beating that little bit faster as he scrambled through the dirt tunnel that led into the Refuge. *No one on watch. Odd.*

He came all the way through to the main chamber, where

hushed secrets filled the air. A circle of monkeys, at least a dozen, huddled round a fire. Joan and Maude were not masked. Trent's skinny shoulders gave him away. The rest he did not know, except Huckster, with his face in full view, who nodded at Claude's arrival and rose to his feet.

"The time is near," Huckster proclaimed. "We must commence with our formal plans. Else we wait at least another twelve moons."

"We are not ready, Tom," said Joan. "You know that in your mind, even if your heart will not allow it."

"What would you have us do?" replied Huckster. "We could spend a lifetime waiting for the perfect circumstances. They'll never come."

Claude pulled up one of the stools, barely making a sound, completing the group of monkeys staring into the crackling fire.

"There is a difference between endurance and idleness." Joan looked around at the others, as if assessing where their hearts lay. "One must avoid the lure of impatience. Just because the Blue Moon is calling doesn't mean logic should be thrown out into the Agumon."

"I do not dismiss logic," said Huckster. "But the time is now. The rains are less. The moon will be strong. An escape is feasible. I know others here feel it too."

"Feelings can lead you astray," said Joan. "This is folly. Good monkeys could lose their lives."

A loud cough came from outside of the circle; a masked male perched in the shadows.

"Do not give too much ferment to fear." He spoke in a soft tone. "Do not spend too much of life fighting feelings. They are a guide, a navigational tool, if you will. And, maybe, for a few, they point away from our trees."

Huckster's head was down as if thinking hard. He lifted it to face the group. "The stars will never align perfectly, Ms Saei. We're better to try now while we have a resolve that is firm. To have tried and failed is better than to have not tried at all."

"The Blue Moon will be full in twenty-eight nights' time," said Maude, joining the conversation. "If the rains are light, as we predict, that is the time to go. The only chance to cross in the next twelve moons—"

"Yes!" said Huckster, leaping onto his stool. "We could talk until the rainforest dries up. But we know the Agumon will be at its lowest level for generations. It's a leap we can finally make. The time has come." He looked around the room, taking in the others, their expressions mirroring his own wide-eyed excitement. "Maya awaits."

Maya?

Joan started again. "Yes, Tom, and it is not a case of a lack of faith when I regret to inform you that I cannot support this plot—if we must talk of feelings, for me the feeling is not right."

"How so?" said Huckster. "What holds us back?"

"I'm not sure we have the numbers to last long outside our canopy," offered Maude. "Nor the experience. The borderbeings would likely devour us, if the State doesn't hunt us down first."

"No," said Joan. "It is not survival out there that concerns me the most. You could bravely travel towards Maya, take all the risks that entails. What I fear most is reality. That place remains a dream. A fantasy. And what of the monkeys back here? Those trying to build a better world, slowly, but surely."

She'll not budge. Stoic? Or stubborn as the frames of Easthaven?

Huckster had fire in his eyes. "What is all *this* for then?" Claude sensed his gaze directed right at him. "We help these hopeful pichus. Help them hear. Help them see. Expose the shadows of our society. Give them something to get behind. And then what? We tell them it's all just an illusion. A story to keep them from boredom. Sit here and wait for the Monvida to fall from the hammock in her royal gardens."

Claude chuckled, leaning forward on his stool, tongue between his teeth.

"Huckster, you do let your emotion cloud your judgement," said Maude. "Joan is not trying to kill the idea completely. We could just do with the fire burning a little stronger. Before we all gamble our lives on a dream."

"It is not just a dream, though, is it …" The same monkey spoke from the shadows; the weight of his voice seemed to enhance the fire, causing a hot flush of air.

Something stirred inside Claude then. *It could be done, a different reality, a quest in search of paradise.*

"I've had my fair share of thinking time lately, up in the Nest," said Huckster. "I've not been idle. The Holy One grows too greedy. Fatter by the day as we feed her and the Acolytes through our subservience. But the State cannot admit that we have gone too far, pushed the rainforest too hard. There are whispers in the trees, unrest is growing, growth is no longer good for everyone. The days of prosperity hang by a loose vine. I, for one, don't want to be around when that vine snaps."

Feet stomped on the ground, fists were shaken, voices rose in anger, and shouts of support rang out. Simple words had sparked a storm. "This isn't some reckless leap from the canopy," continued Huckster, almost shouting, "or a swing blindfolded through the trees. And now, I'll show you why …"

What in the name of Tiarra? A hush fell over proceedings. Huckster went to the board at the back of the chamber, gathering something from the ground. He unfurled what appeared to be a huge piece of parchment, attaching the four corners to the board. *No way? He's been planning this for moons.*

All the monkeys were off their seats, jostling for a better view. A view of a map sketched in thick dark ink. Claude moved closer but hung back a little from the rest. He did not need to look closely; he knew exactly what it showed. And who had taildrawn it. He had seen it only last night. Right at the end of his book.

"That map has been discredited," said Maude. "It's a work of pure fiction."

Claude considered the route in his mind regardless. Over the Agumon at the southern tip of Tierra Libre, down only as far as the flooded forest, Narchia, eastward past the Tangle Tower, back over the river at the abandoned crossing. Before a straight but dangerous course through the unchartered trees they knew only as Shadowbor. Towards a giant waterfall. Aiming always for …

माया

This is Maya! A small beacon of hope, the treasure beyond measure.

Trent gripped Claude's shoulders, shaking him. "You're in, right?" He grinned, a feral look across his features.

Claude brushed him off without agreement. Instead, he turned to depart. The warm, clammy air kept him from clarity. He needed to escape for a moment.

"Next moon we go." Huckster's voice still carried. "You can join. Or you stay behind and let your dreams die along with your conscience."

"Calm, Tom," said Joan. "We meet again next week. We can discuss things properly. See what can be done."

Her words were pointless. The small group stirred again. Arguments flared. Claude took the chance to leave them all behind, crawling his way out into the relative calm of the moonlit rainforest.

A blinking eye waited in the canopy to the south. He turned north, his destination the school, back to what he knew. There was only one thing he wanted now. One thing that would settle his monkeymind. One thing that always worked. A faithful friend.

But even the hallowed wattsplant could not contain his imagination.

The moon cast a shimmering glow across the width of his

temporary residence. He was too awake to try sleeping. His heart still pulsed a rapid rhythm. *An escape plot, unbelievably daring. Can it be done?* He looked out across the school trees and beyond. *Leaving this place—a pichuleap away? It doesn't seem real. And the monkey in the shadows, who was he?*

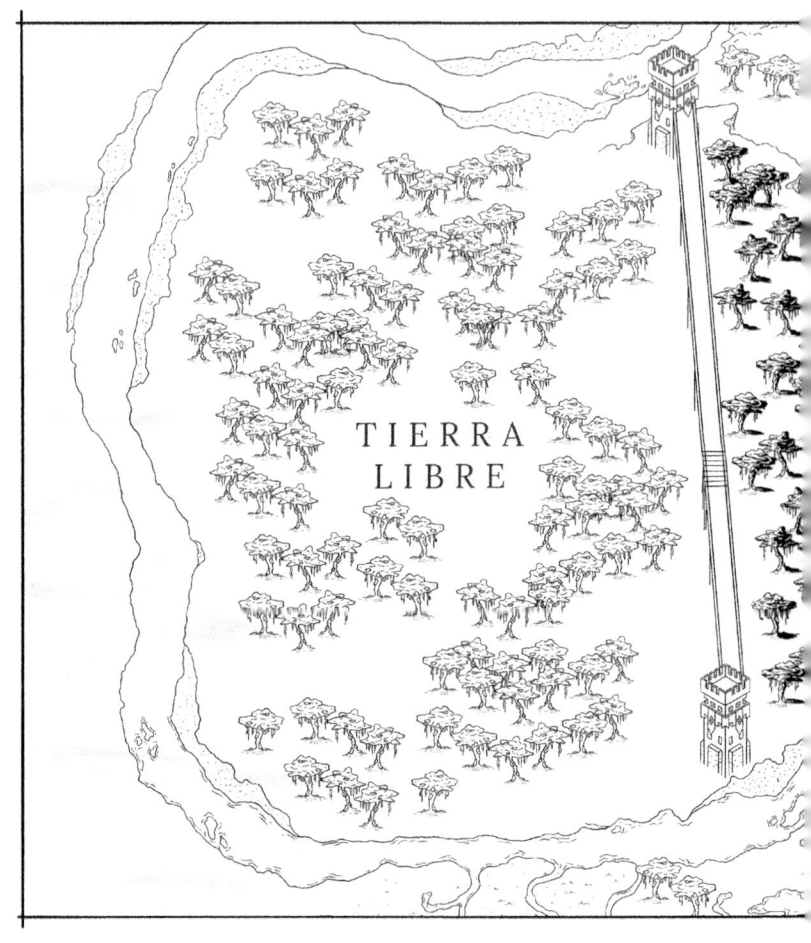

TIERRA
LIBRE

SHADOWBOR

The
Veil

माया

J. Semmelwise Locke

Chapter Fourteen

Curiosity Killed The Capuchin

Efficiency is key. Don't sing, don't dance, don't stray. Just get it done.
Then you can play.

- Monclideus II -

Claude rose before the first whistle, risking an inspection not ordained by the Holy One. He stood in his old tutor room, gazing at the aged portraits of Tierra Libre's previous leaders. From the walls, they beamed back. Assured expressions. Were they all as confident as their paintings portrayed? He was struck by their size, except for Tiarra, of course. Her face pretty, kind and free, while her fur showed faint patches of green.

"A more beautiful monkey I've not seen," said Ms Wald, Claude's old tutor, entering with a stack of books and papers balanced precariously in her arms. "Not that any of us ever saw her. It was told her skin had a shimmering glow under moon or stars. Even brighter by day. Our God of Life. Just beautiful."

"She is beautiful," said Claude. "So delicate. So small, like a wisp of wind might carry her away."

"And some even say she could ride that wind …" Ms Wald chucked down the stack and gathered her coffee press.

He had heard that before—that Tiarra could ride the wind. Float above the darkness of the canopy floor, as light as a woodsprite. Claude had always found this quite curious though. For one reason. There was no wind in Tierra Libre. Barely ever a whisper.

"But alas," said Ms Wald, pouring the dark liquid into two mismatched mugs. "It does not do well to dream of such magic and the Second Emeral is but a mere myth." She slid a mug across the desk. "Coffee, Claude? Do make yourself comfortable."

Squeezing into one of the teeny chairs right in front of her desk, he was grateful for the caffeine and relative calm of the empty classroom.

"I used to work for her, you know?" She pointed at the previous Monvida. "Before she yielded in the sword succession. I got asked to help out with some PR and comms. A difficult job, given her, umm, strong views. However, despite the long hours, it was an honour."

"But you chose to leave the role behind? To become a tutor?"

"Yes," she said. "Hard to believe I know. Eventually I began to crave a simpler existence. A calmer way of life. I now have more time off than most monkeys I know. A decent salary. And I can retire someday soon. When I've saved enough salt, that is." She looked wistfully at Claude. Deep-set wrinkles snaked across her brow and tufts of grey fur sprouted from her ears. Her eyes, though warm, betrayed a bone-deep weariness.

She speaks akin to Karo. How much salt is enough? To do what you actually desire.

"Anyway, enough about me." Ms Wald seemed to break out of a trance. "How's life been since you left the compound? A bright spark like you, already in a respectable position. Can't say I'm surprised. What did you study?"

"I didn't," said Claude. "Shortly after leaving, Mother passed away."

Ms Wald gasped, dousing herself in hot coffee. "Sura? I never knew." She hissed softly, brushing at her damp fur with anxious strokes of her fingers.

"It was hard. Took us time to get our tails back up. I miss her sometimes. Her spirit—"

"Remains within our trees." She paused her fussing, bowed her head, then looked back at Claude. "And what of Tia? She was talented too."

"Uh." *That's one word for it.* "She joined the Acolyte Ascension Programme."

"Something special in that Talador blood," continued Ms Wald. "The mango doesn't fall too far from the tree, as they say. Although I must say that being talented brings its own challenges."

"What do you mean?"

She leant across the table, lowering her voice. "I trust this is in confidence?"

"For my favourite teacher. Of course." He mirrored her action, turning his ear closer.

"Yes, well, the State has insisted on increasing the pool of final year pupils in the Gifted and Talented group. An audition for their utility in the Tribe. A select few will be offered the chance to skip their diplomas and head straight to the upper floors of Hussleton. But something feels amiss. You tell them they're bright and they lose a little fight. Grow entitled. And then when the reality of life hits. It, well, hits them a little harder."

Claude tilted his head. "What might be a better way?"

"I'd scrap the group altogether. I'd give all students an equal chance. Avoid this feeling of them and us. Some in that group scare me a little. Old before their time. Stern and oh-so driven. But what for?"

"For exactly what you said, acquiescence into normal life. Through repetition and constant reinforcement, the pichlets learn how to act as adults. And when the time comes, they know exactly how to fit in."

"Ah, fitting in," chirped the tutor, looking back at the portrait of Tiarra. "The hormiga dream."

Hormigas don't dream. "What do you make of Mr Musk?"

She raised an eyebrow. "Why do you ask?"

"Just curious," said Claude, holding his poker face developed over many long hours in the Cashew.

"I can't say much for my own account." Ms Wald paused. "All I've heard are whispers in the staffroom. Pichlets speaking of odd things for an economics class. And—he's missed a few morning lessons. Found out for the count in his room. Curious, like you say ..."

It still did not make sense. The economics professor was closer to retiree than renegade.

"So, you'd change things here, if you were in charge?"

"Oh, I don't know," she said. "It's a rigorous education system we use. As wooden as the Dormor Trees. A little restricted in terms of what a student can learn. I feel you may have got lucky by missing your diploma."

"Tia got a lot more teaching than me in the end though."

"Maybe," she said, a fond smile softening her features. "She was a most diligent student. But don't forget—there's a huge difference between what you're taught and what you learn. Teaching always comes from the viewpoint of another. True learning? That comes from within."

Her attention drifted back to the portraits. "That's why I love the stories of Fuerza and Tiarra so much. They built everything from nothing, trusting not just in their individual skills but in the abilities of others—and in each other. Seizing opportunities when they came, no matter how small."

The room fell into silence. Daydreams taking them far from the bounds of the school trees. Claude had that opportunity, however slim the chances, for a fresh start. A new beginning. Like all those moons ago with the Hundred.

***

"So, class," Miss Orchid said, "why do we remain within our canopy?"

"The Agumon!" a student blurted out.

"Easthaven!" another shouted.

"They are the hows, not the whys." She took her time, looking from face to face. "Why did we build Easthaven? And why do we spend so much resource maintaining it?"

A hush fell. Some shifted in their seats. Some stared blankly ahead.

Claude was inspecting his next member of the faculty. A less experienced teacher yet supposed specialist in ancient history. Strange given she was younger than he was. He had not been offered a seat, so instead perched on the edge of a table by the door, holding a full view of the room. And Miss Orchid. He pretended to scribble notes on his pad. *She's kind of attractive. Yes, well put together. If you're into the perfectly groomed female fur. She has nice … Focus, Inspector!*

One pichlet ventured, "To keep out what's on the other side."

"Right," she said. "To keep us safe. From the dangers on the other side. Chiefly the borderbeings."

The group erupted into excitable chatter, and she flashed a glance in Claude's direction.

"My mum used to work on Easthaven and saw nuffing," piped up a precocious pupil on the back row. "The whole time, saw and heard nuffing!"

"Nothing." Miss Orchid turned on them. "Do not disdain what lies in the East. Even if your mother did not see it, she will no doubt have felt it. Their power, their presence, their shadows. Many good pichus lost their lives out there. And not deaths of glory, I might add. Deaths of brutality. Limbs ripped off so you wouldn't even recognise them as a monkey."

The pichlet gulped, eyeball to eyeball with the master of the moment. "Okay, Miss," she said, cheeks pure crimson now.

"Yes, take what your parents say with a lick of salt, please."

Maybe not such a fun game after all. Claude assumed that would be the end of it.

However …

"What are they then?" asked another inquisitive soul from nearer the front.

Miss Orchid's slender tail twitched. She looked at Claude again before addressing the collective once more. "The answer to that question is not suitable for this class; there are things we must protect your minds from. And you know what they say about the curious capuchin …"

Silence again. None of the pichlets seemed to get the reference. Claude certainly did.

Miss Orchid continued. "All you need to learn is to be grateful for our Tribe. The safety it provides you. Nothing can threaten you within our trees. Except your own Monkey Business, the poisonous waters of the Agumon, or the howlers."

Sighs echoed; the class exchanged glances loaded with scepticism.

"But, Miss," one said, "what about—"

She cut them off, insisting the matter was settled. A more

daring pichlet delivered a derisive laugh, recognising the complete avoidance of the question. The choice not to explore what the borderbeings were in reality.

She's just like the rest, a hormiga at heart. I'm no longer attracted, despite those … eyes. They really are quite lovely.

***

As evening fell, Claude sat alone in the canteen, nursing a thick soup, supposedly full of nutrients but utterly devoid of flavour. The broth had a strange blueish tint, totally unnatural for the rainforest.

The pupils on the other tables were suspiciously quiet, wearing serious expressions, although who could blame them with what was served up. A few could not keep their eyes from flicking to the inspector. The badge below his chin, clearly sending their stifled imaginations into areas they should not go, watched all the while by the probing eyes of the Monvida. A black-and-white portrait of their current leader consumed a whole section of the back wall.

Claude could not help but wonder about the escape plot. Would she smile and sneer? What if it were pulled off? There would be no half-smile then. And what might she do if it failed and she caught some monkeys in the act? His thoughts churned the blue soup in the depths of his stomach. He pushed the bowl away, not even halfway through, when another landed at its side.

"Good day?" said Tia, slapping him on the back. She dug greedily into her soup. A much greener concoction.

"Uneventful." Claude yawned.

159

"I see," said Tia, not looking up from her bowl. She slurped as she ate.

"You're not eating their stuff?"

"Why in the name of Fuerza would I do that? Have you seen the colour of it?" She peered at Claude's unfinished dinner and burped. "You need to be more careful what you put in your body."

"And you need to be more careful *how much* you're putting in yours."

"Just one of the perks of being an Acolyte." Tia rubbed her belly. A belly that seemed to grow with each passing moon.

"So," she said, focusing on him now, "you hit the gym last night, worked on your leap, and then what?"

"Are you playing mother now, or what?"

"So touchy," she said, tapping her fingertips on the table. "And what are you doing tonight?"

"For crying out loud! I'll do exactly what I want."

"Well, that's not really true, is it?" Tia switched to a hushed tone. "For any of us. We do as we must. You must start to play the game, brother." She paused. "And I've a favour to ask, if that's okay?"

You've got to be kidding me.

Tia shuffled closer on the bench. "It's about Father. He's got wind of the new logging legislation. Something about proposed felling in the Lunaforest."

"And this concerns me how?" Claude was fed up with covering for her employer's conduct. He shuffled himself back

160

to a suitable distance.

"Well," she said unperturbed, "I gather from his note he's quite upset. Needs to talk it out with someone, I think, get it out of his system. Would you mind popping down after we finish up here?"

"Why can't you go? You know more about State regulations than me. Logging in the Lunaforest sounds a pretty bad idea to me too."

"That's kind of the point," she replied. "I think it's better coming from you. I worry if I discuss things with him in too much detail, it may get heated. He doesn't need antagonism at his stage of life."

"I see." Claude curled his tail closer to his chest. "Think I'm your little hormiga now?"

Tia shook her head. "Don't be like one of the pichlets here. I'm asking a favour. Is that really too much to ask one's brother? Once in a blue moon …"

The Blue Moon. How could I forget. Its face will be with us soon enough. He looked at his sister's pleading one. "I'll go see him," he said. "But you'll owe me one. And I want some of that proper food for a start."

"Of course, Claude. I'll speak to the cook now, sort you something proper. I appreciate it." She sprang up and ruffled his fur. He swatted her away like a muddie in a warm dusk.

She arrived back with a hearty bowl of the green-coloured slop, plus a sprinkling of fresh walnuts on top. It was Claude's turn to eat hastily.

Before he had finished, Tia chimed in again. "So I know you'll do a full report tomorrow. But just so I get a sense of things. How's it gone?"

He pushed his bowl away and wiped his mouth. Scanned around the canteen and looked back at her. "Want me to be honest?"

"Naturally," said Tia. "I know what to share and what to keep to myself."

"Well, if you want it for real," he said, "I see fear, I see restraint, and I see boredom. As soon as they're old enough to twiddle a pencil, it's drilled into them that Tuesday through Sunday is for work. Monday for play. But even Monday comes with the warning of No Monkey Business. It's at least one hundred moons in here for them. So that's over four hundred weeks. Four hundred weeks of conditioning! And the worst part is that we only become truly sentient monkeys from age ten. But by this point full programming has already kicked in."

She pursed her lips. "No need to sit on the palisade, brother."

Oh, I have more, sis. "You need permission for a break, permission to eat, permission to tell a joke, permission to swing your tail, permission to hand in your homework, permission to sing, and permission to take a pee. The poor monkeys, they're young minds, not adults. And then, you get them eating this." He pointed at the abandoned bowl of blue that had now curdled nicely.

"It's economical," said Tia, shrugging. "And what about the professors? The ones you're actually here to keep an eye on—"

"I see the same in them too. Fear. Restraint. Boredom. I think they've grown lazy, teaching only from the authorised books and State mandate. Always with a perfectly pruned syllabus to fall back on. There's no personality, no character; they couldn't inspire pichlets even if they were asked to leap across the Agumon blindfolded."

Not my best turn of phrase, given the timing.

Tia stroked her chin, a peculiar look in her eyes. "Is that not the point, though? Pichus need rules to keep their Eyes Forward. Something tangible, structure in their lives. That enables them to be what they need to be."

"If that's really the best way to learn, then yes. But the classes have no interaction. They learn by rote, repetition and memory. How will they apply that in the real rainforest? When novel situations come up. Like the timber shortage or labour trouble with the treepers. We need a few monkeys who can think outside the canopy. These pupils are the future of our Tribe, yet they are all treated like trainee hormigas. Would it not be better if things were a tiny bit more creative?"

"You know what, Claude"—Tia looked round the canteen— "you might be right."

He was speechless. The one thing he had not expected from his sister, the thing he never expected from her, was any form of agreement.

"Maybe there should be more time for creativity," said Tia. "Mould more adaptable pichus. Not for all, of course. But with select individuals, maybe … Yes, I think there could be different ways to get what she wants, what our society needs. Try to distil this in your report."

"Oh, come off it," said Claude. "You know as well as I do, a report won't sway the Monvida."

"Discretion is the better part of valour with her," Tia replied. "However, if you keep it framed nicely. So she can see the benefits clearly. Then you might be surprised."

"I'll write it how I want," said Claude, tiring of the chatter. "I feel I know her now—"

"Ha! You don't know her at all."

Claude smirked. "Forgot you two were best buds."

"You always thought you were the special one," she said. "Yet it was me they named after Tiarra."

"Oh, and you've certainly lived up to her fur. Delicate, glowing, graceful …"

Tia's lips pressed in a thin line. "Just pop down anything suspicious you've noticed with Musky and Orchid."

"There was nothing."

"Well, use some of that creativity you crave then." She looked to the exit. "Do send my best to Father. Dare I say, it might be worth going armed with a batch of that Fuerza-forsaken stuff you like to smoke."

"I'm running low as it happens. You offering?"

"Maybe," said Tia. "If it's for the right cause."

You sly snake. The High Life really does have its perks. They're wasted on you, Tia Talador.

"So this is your payment for my little errand then?"

"As I say"—a devilish glint gleamed in her eye—"for the right cause, there are few things I wouldn't do."

Chapter Fifteen

Dreams Are Danger

*Without dreams of a compelling future, the present can become
a bitter place, lacking any semblance of hope or meaning. Sadly,
pursuing those dreams is not a purely cerebral act. An act of active
defiance is important. Essential even.*

—From "The Seven Core Teachings of Tiarra,"
Chapter One

The waning moon was almost full, which gave a pale lightness to the rainforest on Claude's journey through the trees. He clambered up to the familiar porch, gathering his thoughts, waiting at the entrance to the family treehouse. A home Cama had spent so many moons sculpting to exist in synergy with the surrounding forest. With only one inhabitant these days, it looked a sad, sorry old place now. Weeds had started a battle against the frames. A battle they appeared to be winning. He had not been the same since she left.

Claude rapped his knuckles on the front door.

"Who goes there?" said his father. "Tia, that you?"

"No. It's your other one."

"Claude? What are you doing out at this time?" The door swung open and revealed a very tired-looking monkey. Eyes almost red raw, like a monkey that had not slept in days. Weeks even. "Do you fancy a climb tonight, Claude? I could do with getting out of this tree for a bit." Cama disappeared back into the house. Claude followed without formal invitation.

Once inside, the scene was even more forlorn. A pile of washing up and finished boskies lay unattended, while the smell of dried sweat filled the air.

"Apologies about the mess. I've been working non-stop. Will we need a flame?"

"I think we'll be okay. The moon can guide us."

"Almost full." Cama pointed out of the window towards the sky. "The return of the Blue is nigh."

"It is." Claude was trying not to think about it. "So, what's going on? You've clearly not been sleeping for the past—"

"Few nights. Only a few nights," Cama interrupted, shifting uncomfortably. "I wanted to keep it quiet, didn't want to bother you two. But there aren't many proper pichus you can talk to around here."

Claude could not blame him for that. The Shrouded Grove felt isolated now, even when full of voices. The silence here was not peaceful—not without Sura. It pressed in, wrapping itself around thoughts. Constricting. Tightly.

As Cama continued to faff, fussing with the torch they did not need, Claude found himself drawn to his old bedroom. It was as though the familiar creaks of the treehouse floor were guiding him there.

Moonlight peeked its way in through the same thin slits it always had at this phase, painting lines across the walls.

He brushed his tail along their old bunk beds. Tia's on the top, of course, her, as she had often declared; his below, tucked in the shadow of her pompousness. He could almost hear their whispered voices, trading secrets and small mutinies until Cama's sharp knock on the wall had them scrambling to pretend sleep.

For Fuerza's sake!

How had he not noticed it before?

Sura's dreamcatcher still dangled from its hook at the window. She had made it herself when they were very young, weaving fine root fibres onto a wooden frame. Dreamcatchers were not uncommon in Tierra Libre—their purpose to snare bad dreams while letting good ones pass through.

But maybe Sura's had been different.

This one isn't for keeping dreams away. It's for bringing them to life.

He recalled his mother's words now, clear as if she were right beside him. It had always been there. The unmistakeable shape at its centre.

माया

Claude ripped it off, clutching it in his palm, and returned to Cama; he had finally managed to light the torch. Determination had won. He gripped it in his weathered tail and pointed it out of the family tree.

"Tia sends her best wishes, by the way, but she has *urgent* State business."

"That's fine, she's a busy Acolyte these days."

I'll let that little dig slide. Clearly only one of us can be awarded the divine accolade of busyness.

"I'm sure she's not involved with this," Cama added.

"Let me see it first." Claude gestured for the rough bit of parchment his father held in his thick hands, fingers calloused from decades of hard work.

"Soon there'll be no trees left." Cama cursed, passing it over.

> *Dear Mr Talador (Esteemed treeper),*
>
> *As part of the continued Progress of the Pichu Tribe. The demand for timber continues to increase. We are now developing the fortifications of Easthaven. In response to the risk of violent attacks from Shadowbor and the threat against our faithful monkeys. This is an urgent initiative.*
>
> *The State has therefore taken the decision that logging must occur in the previously protected Lunaforest. All trees on this route are scheduled to be cut down within the next two moons. To satisfy the demands of the Tribe's Defence requirements. Do not worry about re-planting. The soil will be used for State purposes, and exploratory work has*

already begun in another area.

The State would like to put on record their gratitude for the work of all the tree fellers. A small bonus pot is being created. The treeper that brings the most timber in the next two moon phases will be entitled to the reward.

May the fire of Fuerza be with you and your family,

Randall Hopkins (Head of Ecology and Development)

"If I could get my hands and tail on Mr Hopkins," said Cama, "he'd be the first one cut down in this new project."

"I've not heard of him before; no doubt a hormiga covered in townie fur." Claude ripped the parchment and tossed it onto the canopy floor. "I thought you said the Lunaforest has our only untouched trees?"

"It does. And your mother loved that place. We used to …" Cama's expression darkened. "But to improve Easthaven, I guess we can't argue. Where else can we go? There are no other fresh sites in Tierra Libre. The days of the infinite trees are long gone."

"Surely Tia can do something about this?"

"No, no," Cama said, shaking his head. "Don't get your sister involved. I don't want her putting her position in jeopardy."

"This isn't about positions. It's about the future of the Tribe. You said the Lunaforest and its network keep our world healthy.

You must make your dissent known. Surely they'll listen to an experienced worker like you?"

Cama did not answer right away. His silence stretched as they took to the trees, traversing at a slower speed than Claude would have liked.

It took them an age to reach their favourite hollow tree, its cavernous trunk allowing them both to sit. Cama placed the torch into a holder he had fashioned from dried mud and lined with moss. He muttered under his breath about the Lunaforest, his words too low to catch. Claude said nothing, pulling the wattsplant from his pouch. Carefully rolling the paper and feeding in the supply.

The punk soon created a billowing haze that wisped about them with its soothing scent. They passed the pipe between them, watching the spirals crawling their way up into the narrowing trunk. Revealing shapes etched into the bark.

Claude traced the carvings—animals he had never seen. Forms captured by Sura's careful tail. A wolf crouched low, fangs bared in a silent snarl; a jaguar mid-pounce, claws sharp; high up, birds with outstretched wings, their movement almost alive in the torch's glow.

They were more than just carvings. They were lessons of a forgotten world. When Tierra Libre had been home to more than just their kind.

"So what are we going to do about this Hopkins?" said Claude.

"I don't know," said Cama. "There's little we can do. How can we argue with improvements to Easthaven? Your mother—"

"Would be apoplectic!"

"What does that mean?"

"Angry," said Claude. "Ready to challenge them."

Cama shook his head. "I admire your desire, Claude, I really do, to make our world a better place. You get that from her. I share the frustration. Anger too. But when you reach my age, the world takes a different form, and you start to take life a little less seriously. Learn to let things be." He took a deep inhale and exhale.

"You'll just sit here then? Hidden among the trees—the few that are left—waiting for what?"

His father clenched his fists, as if fighting some internal struggle. "I don't know. I need my rest. Bits of peace."

"You can get that when you're dead."

"You're not wrong, son. You're not. I don't mean to discourage your heart. But like I said, I have seen many moons. The reality of life is divorced from the dreams of old. The powers that be have taken our voices, stolen our song. You can fight for what you believe in, and I'm proud that you do." Cama took a long toke. Another sigh. "But, sometimes, however much you want to, you can't change the world. Better to accept what comes to pass. Better to find a place in our Tribe. And, hopefully, some peace. We all must try to face reality, not avoid it …"

Claude snatched back the punk and took a few deep drags. His father had never looked so frail. He had always seemed so strong growing up. Knew so many answers to the questions of life. Now he offered nothing. Nothing at all. Sunken eyelids and a grim and detached expression of a miserable treeper. Apathy all too apparent in the poorly groomed fur.

Getting up, Claude brushed off the ash from his legs. "You've become weak, Father. You've given up. You're forgetting who you were ... what you can still be."

"It is not weakness, Claude. These things are out of our control. We can't do anything about orders of the State." Cama's voice was heavy as he hunched over, tail drooped, seemingly keen to avoid the eyes of his son.

Claude stared at him. "You finish this." He thrust the remaining punk at his father. Cama flinched, the pipe slipping from his grasp, dropping to the ground.

Without another word, Claude turned and clambered out of the hollow trunk.

"Claude, wait!"

"No." He did not stop. "There's nothing more to say." He looked for a route into the canopy.

"Claude?" Cama pleaded. "There's another reason I don't resist. It's too late. The Lunaforest is already alive with the sound of trees hitting the ground. All the treepers are after the reward. There's nothing—"

Claude was already climbing, the moon his guide, Cama's words lost to all but the insects of the night.

***

"I was hoping I'd see you here soon," said Huckster as he raised his nose from a book. He was sitting among the bookcases of the Refuge, feet by the fire, beckoning for Claude to join him. "How's my favourite inspector?"

"Angry."

"I see," said Huckster. "Anything I can help with?"

"Not unless you have a direct vine to the Monvida," said Claude, slumping into the other seat beside the fire. "How are you anyway?"

"Thoughtful." Huckster flashed him the cover. "I'm making my way through *The Ordinary Pichu – A History of Work*"—he turned it over to the back—"by Aldous Musk."

"Dry."

"A tad." Huckster laughed. "Interesting though. And here's a question for you: Guess how many hours our ancestors worked back near the genesis of our Tribe?"

"No idea." It was a delightful minimum of eighty-four hours now, he knew. "Seventy-odd?"

"Lower."

"Fifty."

"Not even close." Huckster smiled, putting the book on the floor and picking up the tongs hanging beside the fire. "Come on, a bright monkey like you can get it …"

Claude raised his hands and tail. "Twenty-five?"

"Warmer," said Huckster, poking at the embers and shuffling a few logs.

"Twenty?"

"Exactly!" said Huckster at the exact same time a crackle of ash fired past them. "Twenty hours, Claude. Thousands of moons ago. That many hours of work to provide themselves with enough food, water, shelter and supplies. The rest was given up to living life. Unadulterated play. Tree climbing in the Lunaforest, star watching, reading, as much as you liked."

"Sounds like paradise."

"Sounds like it was. Maybe that's what's waiting for us at Maya. One can almost taste it, no?"

"I guess." *He certainly sells the dream. But is he too far from reality, like some of them say?*

Huckster paused before lowering his voice. "Have you had a chance to think about your own involvement in our plan?"

"I've thought of little else." Claude slouched back in the chair. The escape plot had put a rift the size of the Agumon through the Refuge. Huckster had been branded both messiah and fool. Some favoured the former view, others the latter. Some even left the group at once. Never to be seen again. The dangers too grave, the implications too real. Who could blame them?

"Must we go this moon?" asked Claude.

"Well, it is the Blue Moon, after all. And I don't really fancy another twelve under our current leader."

"Is she really any worse than those before her?"

"Exactly." Huckster leant forward, speaking more quickly. "That is *the* problem. Nothing changes. Nothing improves. All her talk of Eyes Forward, it's a smokescreen. Acquiescence is danger."

Claude nodded.

"You're not a fan of hers, are you?" Huckster pressed.

"I have nothing personal against her. But I cannot say I warm to her, and I loathe the world she rules over. What she has created for the ordinary monkey." Claude took a look behind him as if Tia, or a hormiga, could be lurking. "I do not trust her." *And never will.*

"So where will you put your trust?" said Huckster, rising to chuck on fresh firewood. It took light rapidly.

Is there any monkey you can trust if your father's given up? "I trust most of the pichus here," said Claude. "Joan, Maude and you."

"I am grateful for that. Sadly the trust of Ms Saei has not been enough to convince her of any involvement. A wise mogician would have been of great value outside our forest no doubt." He sighed. "Maude has changed her tune slightly though, saying she would find it hard not to join. And yet our provisional party numbers ten. You could be the eleventh, Inspector. A wonderful chance. A chance to go beyond the mist, a dangerous but thrilling adventure in search of paradise. We could climb in the wild and sing songs of old together. A bold pichu like yourself would fit in nicely. You have some of the green in you, that would give us all hope. Now I would trust to that."

A flame crackled as Huckster looked into Claude's eyes. The older monkey's shone hazel in the firelight. The deep determination of someone who had waited for their big chance and knew the moment was nigh. "Can I count on you, my friend?"

Claude returned the gaze. Wanting to be the monkey Huckster thought he was capable of being. "My mother died out there, you know?"

"A borderbeing?"

"Yup."

Huckster recoiled. "You'll need even more courage than the rest of us then. Although, there are a few who claim those shadow creatures are not quite as the State makes out. It's a risky venture no doubt. Your caution is no sin. Do not fret, sleep on it a little longer."

Huckster gripped Claude's shoulder. "I only ask now as the Blue Moon will not wait for any pichu, it will soon loom large. Some opportunities come before one is ready." He released his grip. "Cor! Get me, the preacher. I'll not force this plot on any pichu. This is up to you." Huckster opened his book again. "Now, give me a chance to read alone awhile. For I, too, must face up to my fears."

Another crackle spat from the fire, landing on the back of Claude's tail with a sizzle. He sat for a while then, staring into its centre, tired yet alert. Not knowing whether the fire in his heart was as strong.

Chapter Sixteen
The Myth Of Retirement

Facing the real within reality is often the hardest route to climb. We are drawn to stories that provide comfort. Not tales that challenge us to move.

- Cama Albert -

As with all big life decisions, Claude found himself tackling things in the way many monkeys do. Avoiding them.

He inadvertently found himself giving the Refuge a wide berth, in the same way one did the poisonous waters of the Agumon. Out of fear, or a more sensible monkeymind, he did not know. However, there was no escaping the call, even as he buried himself in the work of Floor 9. Each evening, Trent would be waiting for him outside the turnstiles. Each evening, Claude pushed him away and returned peacefully home. Each evening, Trent would point to the moon without words. It was waxing. Not long before the Blue ...

Claude was sweating already as he slinked down to the

Dormor 43 kitchen. He hissed at a pair of other early risers, too close to where he wanted to be. Snatching yesterday's roast, he heaped three spoonfuls into his mug, the rest spilling over the counter. Ignoring the mess, he hastened back to his pod.

The caffeine hit hard and fast, and he began to shuffle round his home. His monkeymind shuffling too. *Should I go with Huckster? Should I tell Karo and Beena? And Father—should I mention it to him? Was I too hard on him that night?* The questions kept coming. *Why do things get harder the more you think about them?*

A rap of knuckles against wood reverberated through his pod.

How strange. He never got visitors. Claude clambered over to the periscope on his door. A tall, thin pichu with neat box-cut fur waited. The Acolyte from the night he sought to forget.

The plot's over! It's been discovered, or the Refuge has …

"Talador, you ready?"

"Two ticks." Claude downed his coffee. He then shoved his punk and the copy of *In Search of* माया under his pillow. "Only just had my morning brew, you know. What's your business?"

"The Holy One's," they said. "Hurry up."

Claude half opened the door. Close up, his visitor looked like a monkey who experienced every day as one big chore. A battle to get through. One he would no doubt win. Yet a chore all the same.

"Bain Longtail," he said. "Nice to meet you."

Reluctantly, Claude unfurled his tail, meeting the sharp-tipped one extended towards him. Their brief link sent a sudden painful jolt through his body that left him teetering on the edge of his pod. He reeled backwards, clutching the doorframe. Without so much as a glance back, Bain climbed straight down to the ground. Huffing, Claude slid the bolt into place, locking his door, and followed after him.

In the kitchen, Dubbert muttered while scrubbing the worktop; with each swipe of the cloth, he edged closer, shooting a suspicious glare at the pair. Bain paid him no heed and addressed Claude. "You'll have the honour of spending the day with me today."

Dubbert snorted, cloth pausing mid-swipe. He was practically at his elbow now. Not even pretending anymore. Claude resisted the urge to shove him.

"I was just about to set off for Floor 9, actually. Need to write up my latest report on the initial Lunaforest yield—"

"Won't be needed," said Bain. "It's all been covered. We had a round table with the Holy One last night. Your inspection services are needed today. I understand that's what you prefer?"

"Well, yes, Longtail, I just …"

"Perhaps, Talador"—Bain stepped forward, casting a shadow over them—"you just need to listen a bit more."

What a twit.

"We'll head northwest, near the Agumon," continued Bain. "To the Retirement Village. It's about time you went there, isn't it, Talador?"

Claude's snicker escaped, unsure if that had been a joke. Bain smiled, showing perfect white canines. "Shall we?" He pointed away from the normal track to Hussleton.

Behind him, Dubbert had stopped scrubbing and was now rustling a fresh copy of the *Pichugraph*. "Don't forget your friends on Floor 9, Claude."

Friends?

***

Bain set a hard pace, and they soon reached a narrow path laden with bark and flanked by carefully cropped figs and palms.

"Your mission is simple in its scope," Bain said, leading them forward. "Tricky in its implementation. You're here to see if anyone is a disruptor. A danger to the peace. There's been rumours of a troublemaker who goes by the alias of 'Freemon'. Singing forbidden songs, flaunting regulations and spreading dissent amongst the inhabitants."

Claude nodded. *Sounds like a few monkeys I know …*

"Keep your eyes open and report back to me if you see anything suspicious."

"Naturally," said Claude as they rounded the bend, the path opening up to reveal a wider vista. A large organised area of buildings and expertly cultivated foliage. Sprinklers combined with the dew on the ground to keep things an unusually luscious green.

Bain gestured towards the entrance. "Be discreet, don't draw attention to yourself. And whatever you do, don't mention you're here on behalf of the Holy One."

As Claude traversed the inner halls of the village, he thought he had seen more dissent among the hormigas than this rabble of fossils. Most of the monkeys were propped up in big wooden armchairs. Blank expressions fixed on their faces. No work, no crosswords, no games, no smiles, no conversations, no life, it seemed. A band of nurses buzzed around, caring for the large number of occupants.

Not quite the paradise Karo described.

A stench hit Claude, on par with the Dump. He tried desperately not to hold his nose or breathe in too much stale air, hurrying to the gardens.

At least outside a few pichus possessed a pulse. The old bat from the Agumon waved her stick around like a sword, cursing something, someone or some god. She then spoke to a white-furred monkey, who looked up at her from a back so hunched he could almost lick the ground. Claude nodded to them in passing, but they were too engrossed in discussing the dinner menu.

Another monkey moved in perfect circles, just out of reach of the sprinklers, a pace those at the Commute would have been proud of. Claude counted five laps, without a break, and onwards. Why he kept going round, Claude could not say. He did not much care either.

A cough echoed through the grounds; a monkey sat in the shade at the outer edge, gazing out at the fenced-off rainforest. He had a book on his lap—*The Verdan Emeral.* And unlike the others, he did not have any medical staff in the immediate vicinity.

Claude ambled over. The monkey seemed to be quoting old nutball stats. Muttering away.

"Mind if I take a seat, sir?"

The old pichu's eyes flickered towards Claude's badge. A flash of a smile. A crooked one, numerous battered teeth. A genuine smile all the same. "You here on behalf of the State?" He had a gruff tone.

"In a manner of speaking," said Claude.

"Nicely put. Well, please pass on my feedback—that their so-called paradise—is in fact a stinking dung hole."

"That good, hey?"

A snigger. "Who are you then?"

"Name's Claude Talador and I'm here looking for …" He switched to a whisper. "A disruptor of the peace."

The old monkey's voice crackled with irony. "What a wonderful thought. Peace getting disrupted. Here!" Another coughing fit racked his body.

"You can get something for that, you know?"

"Oh, I know, Mr Talador. But I don't trust all those hormigas. Never have, never will. Soon as a retiree gets ill here, they stick 'em on a load of pastes. All different flavours. Supposed to cure your ailments. But you know the funny thing? It certainly doesn't cure 'em! It makes them worse. Lost a few good friends here. If you can call them that. Put their trust in the hormigas. And the snakes finished them off in their sleep."

"I somehow doubt that—"

"A figure of speech." He scoffed. "Not literally. Although now I think of it, I wouldn't be surprised."

"Curious," said Claude, noting the monkey's sunken cheeks

and gaunt frame, his bones jutting from beneath scraggly fur. *Clearly suspicious of authority. Not the worst thing in this world. Rare though.* "And how's the food?"

"No, no, no." The old monkey grinned. "Don't get me started on that."

He's going to anyway. This monkey likes the sound of his own voice. That, or he doesn't get to use it much.

"I mean, my eyes aren't what they were, but you should see the slop they feed us. Swear it's gone blue. Ain't natural, Mr Talador. Most of the villagers lap it up like a bosky on the day of rest. But there's something evil in that stuff. Starts to break down your defences. You eat it. It eats away at your systems. I feed off scraps. Bits I can get from the staff plates, leftovers, you know. A pichu's gotta do what a pichu's gotta do."

Claude's ears perked. He crouched down beside the monkey. "You really hate the hormigas then?"

"Why you asking?" The old monkey flashed another crooked grin. "Trying to set me up, Mr Talador?"

"Quite the opposite." Claude uncrossed his arms and let his tail hang loose. "I'm here to learn, sir."

"Why I never." He shook his head. "You seem a little different to the rest. Some weird fur you've got there. Anyone ever told you that?"

"No. You're the first." Claude rolled his eyes at the old pichu's hoots of delight.

"Woah, you can stay," he chortled. "You can stay!"

Claude switched to a quieter tone. "So, sir, why don't you tell me what you really think of this place?"

"How long you got?"

"About five more minutes," said Claude, looking back at the village, expecting the appearance of Bain at any moment.

"Oh, that should do it. Well, make yourself comfy. It's some really good shit. As tasty as that blue slop." And the old monkey licked his lips. "So, the secret of the village is the secret of all great charlatans. You know any charlatans, Mr Talador?"

"Not personally."

"Well, charlatans are a rare breed of monkey, canny mind and well-groomed fur. In many ways your average pichu. Only they can be oh so powerful. Oh so dangerous. And the thing is, the village is one big charlatan, big as the Monvida after a feast. What I'm sure you'll see is monkeys are desperate to make their way here. They've scraped, they've saved, they've forgone. All those long weeks in the office are worth it. The lovely ripe mango at the end of a long climb. Life may be a drag, but it'll be worth it in the end. All the while you tick closer to retirement. The moon of your life gets fuller. The prospect then starts to look like bliss." He put a hand on Claude's arm, gripping it, bringing him closer. "You've even heard that term used, I'm sure, a time when you might finally be able to put your tail up. No cares, no worries. No more howlers, no early morning commute, no more late nights of brain fog. Oh how you look forward to the freedom of retirement. You with me, Mr Talador?"

"I am," said Claude. *The story Karo and Ms Wald eat up like fresh bugslaw.*

"Then here's the thing. A few lucky monkeys make it this far. The letter from the State arrives at the door with a short thanks and a welcome to the village. Please shut up shop and potter your way over there. The feeling is like nothing else. Unadulterated excitement. Paradise a pichulength away. You head inside here, all excited, smelling the figs, taking in the view of the lush greens. Then boom! It hits you." His eyes went wide. "Like the nub of a well-told joke. Because you take a seat in a comfy chair and some friendly-looking nurse comes over—time for that foot rub, a nice good coffee and a nap. Oh, no, no. They shove some of that blue slop at you, tell you to sit in silence, order you to your smelly bedroom before you even see the moon. And then you just lie there. Lie there with no fur or grey as a grub. You can't get your tail up, have a rotten prostate and if you're lucky, one or two teeth wobbling in your feeble gums. Clinging to your mouth, like you've been clinging to life. See, look." He wobbled a canine enthusiastically. "No, the village is no paradise, far from it. It's closer to purgatory. Your moon is not waxing, it's on the wane. Last jump before—well—you know …"

He paused, looking out at the jungle, then back to Claude. "Where's the charlatan in all this you may ask? Well, as the hormigas swarm around your old friends who are now deaf, blind and dumb, you start to realise there is no mango. But the charlatan, the State, has got what they wanted from you. Decades of labour, taxes and muddie bites. Now all they need to do is get rid of you as soon as is safe. A pile of bones at the Dump, ashes sprinkled in the sodden ground or tossed in the Agumon. Sooner the better. Either way, it's only a matter of time. Everyone here's so frail. So lifeless. The charlatan is already out hooking the next victim. Straight from boarding school. Ready to make another sale."

"Selling what exactly?"

"The myth of retirement, Mr Talador!" The old monkey cackled, breaking into another almighty coughing fit. This one seemed to have no end.

Claude got up gingerly; he could not help but admire the cunning of the system. Get pichus to inflict their own restrictions and morality and there is little need for strict authoritarianism. By worshipping the divinity of the Monvida, they have something to trust. Making life less challenging, removing the need to search for meaning, all the while clinging onto the vine-like promise of paradise. The chance to go to *this* place.

"Thank you, sir," Claude said eventually. "I appreciate your honesty."

"Ain't no point in lying. You're going to report me now, I guess? Label me as a disruptor of the peace."

"That you are. But no, I'm not here to report you. Like I said, I'm here to learn."

"Well, consider this your education. Can't tell you how much I wish I'd known what this place was really like before I signed the lease. Could've escaped while I still had a working tail. Before I'd faffed away five hundred moons in a stuffy office full of leeches and jobsworths!"

"Where did you work?"

The old monkey checked his pouch, fumbling with crooked fingers. He pulled out a battered old pass, no longer on a lanyard. Worn to obscurity, Claude recognised it all the same.

"I was an inspector too."

"Well I never." Claude squinted at the badge, the name erased. "Mr—"

"Freemon," said the pichu with a wink. "The one free monkey still left in this place."

They shook tails, and a final coughing fit ravaged the retiree. Bain, now patrolling the front of the gardens, glanced over.

"Thank you, Mr Freemon," Claude said.

The old monkey looked peaceful for the first time. Probably the most content he had been in years. It was off his chest, and he had tried to help someone. Freemon closed his eyes then, humming a tune. A very old song, "Tiarra of the Trees".

Claude left him to his tranquillity, meeting Bain at the edge of the gardens. The staff seemed unconcerned by their presence. The inhabitants oblivious.

"Any luck rooting out the dissenter?" the Acolyte asked.

"Nope," said Claude. "All seem a pretty washed-out bunch to me. No disruptors I can see."

"What about that one?" Bain signalled at the old female. "Been known to sneak out, apparently."

"Nope, a little crazy, but wouldn't be able to start a fire in a burning forest."

"Excuse me?"

"A phrase, Longtail."

"Right." Bain tipped his head in the direction of Freemon. "And that one?"

"Even crazier," Claude offered without hesitation. "The pichu in question must be operating stealthily. I'd need more time to uncover their movements."

"I see. I think we'll leave it there for now." Bain seemed to study him for a second. "Shame really. I thought a monkey of your supposed talent might have picked up on such a character quite quickly. I guess *her* faith is misplaced."

If only he knew.

"Anyway, time you got back to Floor 9," Bain continued. "You can finish off that Lunaforest report before the final whistle. Oh, and she wants to see you tomorrow. Report to the TVA reception at first light."

Claude twitched. "What for?"

"Good news, I believe, Talador. Good news indeed."

Chapter Seventeen
The Badge Of Stress

You can spend your whole life longing for what is just out of reach.
The perennial pursuit of the next thing. Losing grip on what is.

- Hans Sehnsucht -

Claude hunched in his cubicle and composed the note for the third time. But for the third time, he scrunched it up and chucked it straight in the bin. He really hoped she would consider a stop to the felling in the Lunaforest. Or at the least, vow to leave a few strong trees still standing. However, the more he tried to write it, the more he thought of Tia's words about how you must sweeten it for the Monvida. Sell the benefits of any suggestions. Mentioning that there would soon be no trees left in Tierra Libre did not quite fit that brief. Maybe his father was not such a fool after all. Politics was a prickly profession, one not suited to his temperament.

"Oh, stuff it," said Claude, snatching a few boskies from the secret compartment beneath his desk. He swivelled off his chair and dangled one in front of Beena. "Quick break, Ms Maitri?"

Engrossed in the ever-growing pile of papers before her, she shook her head, nose buried in presumably organised chaos.

"Suit yourself." Claude turned away and moved over to Karo's office. He rapped on the door and waited. No answer. "Fine then!" he grumbled and made his way out of Floor 9 and down to the outdoor break zone.

A wave of despair washed over him; he had timed it terribly. The skies darkened, unleashing a monsoon through the trees at the base of Hussleton. He perched beneath a wide palm as the rain pounded the floor, creating deep brown pools.

What could the Holy One want from me tomorrow? Right before the Blue Moon. Surely it can't be …

"Stop it." Claude brushed his thoughts aside and turned his attention to the two hormigas standing guard. He edged a little closer to their whips. Just in range. Yawned, deliberately loud, and flicked a dash of bosky ash in their direction. The attack was instant. A fierce swipe at his back. He cartwheeled out of the way, avoiding it with ease. With a quick bow to the pair, he rushed back through the turnstiles.

Settling back into his cubicle, he plonked his earplugs back in and started a new task. Ordering his inspection papers. He could almost feel himself drifting off …

"Claude!"

He lurched forward, snapping his pencil on the desk, head whipping towards the cry. A crowd had formed right outside

Karo's office. *What in the name of Tiarra?*

"Claude! Come quick!"

As Beena's voice rang out, he bolted from his desk, almost tripping over his tail. He got stuck behind a few colleagues, including Dubbert, rushing towards the commotion. A herd of townies formed a blockade. Claude shoved his way through, without a care for who he offended, bursting through the door.

She trembled in the corner, arms curled around herself, eyes holding a haunted gaze. Medical hormigas knelt over a prone Karo. Their hands moving urgently, pumping his chest. A frantic rhythm.

Claude wrapped his arms around Beena as she gasped, burying her head into his fur. He kept one eye on Karo, as the medics continued to work. The minutes dragged on. The medics slowed, then stopped, looking at each other without emotion. An exchange of nods. Then one signalled a hand across their throat.

Holy shit! The poor chap's already gone.

Beena shrank, a muffled sob breaking free as her legs buckled. Claude gripped her tighter, holding her upright as the hormigas silently departed. Leaving behind the harsh stillness of loss.

Karo's body lay flat on his private office floor.

Outside, the excitable chatter of the onlookers swelled.

Gently letting go of Beena, Claude turned towards the door, tail primed. "Is this some sort of sport for you? Are your lives so sterile that you take enjoyment from this?"

He slammed the door in their faces. Aggressive knocks followed. Jabbering voices.

Yet he did not really hear them. Beena crouched over, shoulders heaving as she struggled to get her breath. Claude moved to Karo, checking for a pulse.

None.

He pressed a hand to Karo's brow, pausing before easing his eyelids shut. He straightened up his friend's fur, a fragment of dignity, noted an unusual level of calm on his face.

"Take it steady, friend," Claude said quietly. "May you find light beyond the mist."

The office door smashed open. A fresh batch of hormigas brushed Claude aside. He retreated, slumping next to Beena, watching glumly as things concluded. The hormigas worked quickly but with great difficulty, levering Karo onto a bamboo stretcher. The spectators crowded together, an unruly mass of bodies vying for a better view. A hubbub of excitement and chatter. They had not seen Monkey Business like this in many a moon. If ever.

"The stress," said Beena. "He said it'd be the death of him."

"And so close to retirement," muttered Claude, nursing her head on his shoulder. "Slowly, slowly, catchy monkey."

Chapter Eighteen

Staring At The Status Quo

All monkeys call themselves honest. But can they tell the truth in all situations? Can they stick to their principles in the light of temptation? What about when their life is on the line?

- Jorgina Wellor -

Claude settled into a chair in a dome-shaped waiting room, gazing out its window towards the myriad of small pools and intricately channelled rivers that comprised the Spas of Banderflow. A cool water relaxation centre, costing thousands of grams of aethersalt, reserved for the elites.

With a sigh, he sipped his coffee and closed his eyes. A fan's firm breeze, a privilege of those at the Treetop of Valiant Ascendance, tousled his fur. Opening them again, he spotted the *Pichugraph* on the table. He thumbed through the newspaper, unable to see what he was looking for. Skimming through articles of dross and irrelevancies. It was not until the final page. Or just before it. The article was short, tucked in among the obituaries.

FORTY-SIX-YEAR-OLD WORKER DIES OF UNDIAGNOSED HEART CONDITION — INSURERS TO ISSUE FAMILY WITH LARGE DEATH IN SERVICE COMPENSATION PACKAGE.

Mr Karo Shi (46), a townie who had worked as an official State Inspector for over twenty years, was found dead in his private office by colleagues yesterday afternoon. Medical hormigas rushed to the scene but he had suffered a fatal myocardial infarction.

The autopsy revealed Mr Shi had a pre-existing heart condition that had not been picked up by Hussleton Workers Health Co (HWHC). A spokesmonkey for HWHC said that it was unfortunate that the condition had not been detected at the annual review only six weeks before. However, they added that although the developments of medical science are progressing rapidly, there are still certain anomalies of the monkey body that can escape the ninety-nine point nine percent accuracy of their reviews.

HWHC passes on its condolences to Mr Shi's family and friends. His wife will receive a large fee, staggered over the next six moons. The hope is this can go some way to easing the loss of a devoted father and loyal employee.

Claude's certainty about Karo's death not being the result of a pre-existing condition remained. He smelt a vampire bat. A large one too. *The poor buffoon died of one thing: stress.* Constant stress and anxiety had overclocked his friend's body.

His mind raced. The idea of a clandestine arrangement between the State and the HWHC seemed plausible. And the *Pichugraph*'s involvement ... if they took the rap, there would undoubtedly be some worthwhile concessions, or most likely a cut to their corporation tax. Financial gains often led to shady deals; he had witnessed it countless times before.

And the irony! Without Karo around, Bo Shi and the pichlets would be better off than ever before. The SI had squandered any aethersalt he got his hands on. At the Cashew Casino, at the stadium, at one of the taverns, lining the State's coffers. He doubted their financial stability would provide much solace. He knew the void left by a parent's absence all too well. Three pichlets growing up without a father!

"Mr Talador, she'll see you now," said a hormiga. "Please see my colleagues at the lift."

He placed the paper aside.

Two hormigas waited by a winch, and they nodded to him. One gestured inside to a box made of dark glossy wood. The doors snapped shut behind him; grunts followed as the hormigas cranked him up towards the very top of the citadel. Claude glanced down at his fur—tidier than normal. Beena had done her best to sort out the knots. He was not even angry. He was bitter, down to the core. A steely determination had settled overnight.

The lift bell dinged, and the doors were opened. Claude was assaulted by stunning brightness. A hint of cool air too, carrying with it the lush scent of dawn. The deep orange sunlight glinted off verdant treetops, highlighting a section of life stubbornly clinging on. But beyond, scars of destruction marred the view— expanses of barren canopy and skeletal trees stripped bare. From this height, the contrast was stark—the beauty of the luvé clashed with the reality of a rainforest fighting to thrive once more. *Does she not see this?*

"Welcome to my actual office," said the Monvida, splayed out across a huge cushioned sofa. She tapped idly on the armrest, exuding an air of power. Four armed guards flanked her, each with blank expressions. A fan hummed softly, its breeze ruffling a bundle of papers on the small table in front of her, held down by a wobbling wooden totem shaped like a monkey face. Fuerza's. Next to it, another table held the trappings of indulgence—a bottle, two goblets, and a half-eaten fruit platter. The sofa creaked as she plucked a juicy-looking jaboticaba and popped it into her mouth. Claude's gaze flicked to one of the hormigas; he half-expected them to offer to feed her by hand.

He fidgeted closer. Yet his eyes were drawn away from her to the panoramic view of the canopy. *How the other half live.*

"Not a place for monkeys scared of heights," she said, raising herself to a more formal seating position, "like most of our pichus are … But quite a view, don't you think?"

"It is impressive," he said.

"Why, thank you, Talador. The structure of the TVA was built from the finest timber. Hundreds of monkeys were involved in its construction. It was the designers though, who insisted on the views. What great talent we have within our borders—those treepers certainly know their classical architecture. Just a shame the trees are no longer infinite." The Monvida paused, playing a pick through her teeth. "But we have plans for that. Ways to keep growing. As long as those borderbeings stay quiet ..."

Claude tipped his head. She beckoned for the hormigas to depart with a click of her fingers. He noticed Flameré, the famous sword, hanging behind her in its sheath. A bead of sweat formed and trickled down his forehead, betraying his usual state of casual indifference. He flicked it off as if a dead bug on the shoulder.

"Fans not strong enough for you?" The Monvida laughed. "Well, it's not every day you get a taste of the High Life, is it?"

"You're not wrong."

"Drink?" She gestured to a flask containing a dark red liquid.

The scent was clear. Fig ferment. "I'm okay," he replied.

"As you please." She took a generous sip from her goblet. "I have good tidings for you today, Talador. But I understand there is some bad we must discuss first. Your colleague from Floor 9. Terrible shame. My condolences. I understand you were close?"

"We were." His brows furrowed as he conjured up the image of them that night at the inn. What Karo had said. He swallowed. "He was taken too soon."

"The Balban Reaper can bring its blade to bear at any moment," she said. "And the Reaper does not discriminate, it seems."

So it seems, Your Holiness.

"Anyway, Eyes Forward," the Monvida proclaimed. "Are you ready? To make the leap. To better serve your fellow pichus. The next stage in your fledgling career?" She flicked through some papers in front of her. "Reports of your work are solid. A sharp mind. But easily distracted at times. A little idealistic. Does that sound fair?"

Where've those labels come from? They're spot on. "Not necessarily bad traits?"

"No, not necessarily. We will have to be careful, though." Her eyes bored into him. "So you may have already guessed why you are here. It is the evening of the Blue Moon tomorrow and the southern stars will shine bright."

His tail twitched without warning.

"To mark this occasion, I will be having a gathering of the Acolytes. We will see in the new moon. And talk of strategy, the future and our dreams." She stopped, tipping her goblet in his direction, licking her lips in a too-obvious fashion. "Should be right up your tree, Talador. There will be entertainment, delicious food aplenty and even a bit of ferment …"

"But it's a work night." The words came out before he could stifle them.

"It is, you are right." The half-smile arrived. "But I thought by now, after your inspections, you would have learnt that things are not always what they seem. One must scratch a little beneath the bark."

"That's true."

"Meaning?"

He closed his eyes for a second. The eye of the bird flashed into his mind, then flew over the Agumon. He looked at her again, cleared his throat. "I have seen this Tribe has many problems. Problems that have always been swept away. Beneath the bark, as you say—"

"And what problems do you mean?"

"The Dump. The Pen. The Boarding School. The Retirement Village. Pretty much everywhere I've been these past moons." He fidgeted about in front of the Monvida like a monkey confined. Turning to face her, he added, "The State must do more. We must help ordinary monkeys more. Instead, we focus on ourselves. Our own pods. But look what happened to poor Karo. And his family. They carry the cost."

Claude's face started to feel hot as the Monvida's eyes widened, her gaze pinning him in place with an unsettling intensity. Her lips parted, as if to speak but then closed again.

"I suppose you think I'm heartless, don't you, Talador?"

Yes! The word hovered on his tongue. "No, Your Holiness, I just think things must change."

The Monvida looked ready with her riposte, but—

"Mother, what's going on?" The voice was light, curious and young. A pichlet, probably no older than thirteen, peeked into the room. Her face was kind, her manner mild. "It's getting very hot up here," she said, fanning herself.

"Don't worry, dearest. We will go to the spa soon. Cool off."

"When?" A quiet impatience.

"Soon, darling." The Monvida's tone had transformed into something altogether different. A certain softness. Jarring from her. "Mum just has a matter to attend to first."

The pichlet nodded, then cast a glance at Claude, offering up a tiny smile. "Can we play when you're done? Or go to the lower levels? You did promise."

The Monvida hesitated, a flicker of conflict. Then it was gone, replaced by her usual control. "We will see," she said, a touch too firm. "Get back to your studies, please."

The little monkey's smile dimmed before she turned, skipping off into the unknown reaches of the TVA. A couple of thin streaks of red lined the short fur of her back. Before Claude could make sense of it—

"Where was I, Talador?" The Monvida picked up a piece of fruit, squeezing it between her thumbs. "Change is a juicy mango, that is true. Only, it is not as straightforward as most pichus think. You are naive, Talador. There are things about this world you do not know. Things you could not even comprehend." She grabbed the Fuerza totem. It had neither legs nor tail. She rolled it from side to side on the table, picking it up and showing it to Claude. "Do you know what this symbolises?"

He shrugged.

She thrust it towards him. "Here, hold it."

He caught it awkwardly, its weight catching him off guard. A subtle heat spread through his fingers. The face of Fuerza stared back at him, red-painted eyes flickering with a strange inner light. Creating a soft yellow luvé glow around them. He placed it back on the table, watching as it wobbled. The Monvida leant in, gave it a nudge and then another, harder this time. She shoved it once more, trying to knock it over. Only the totem defied her, righting itself each time.

"As long as the weight is strong enough," she said, "you cannot topple it. That is the trick. And that is our Tribe, Talador. The belief of ordinary monkeys is what keeps it upright."

"What if we don't want to stand all the time?" he replied. "What if we want to go back to our roots? Climbing again?"

She scoffed. "I admire your ambitions, Talador. Even if they are a little lofty. It convinces me even more that it is time for you. Your chance to really make a difference, work on these problems. At the party tomorrow, I would like to officially welcome you." The half-smile returned with aplomb.

"Welcome me to what?"

"Come on, you are not *that* naive ..." She cackled. "I am inviting you to follow your sister. Become an Acolyte. The chance to make your family proud."

Claude's mouth dropped. He immediately snapped it shut. "I've not been an inspector that long. I—"

"Talent has no age limit," she said. "We think you are ready.

You can leave the stuffy confines of Floor 9 and come join us here. It is a bit cooler working conditions as you can tell. Plus, you will get a new pod, a bit more power, the High Life. Even a chance to change things, like you suggest. What do you say?"

What can I say? This is madness. Claude looked to the ceiling. Then to the floor. Only an instant passed. More than enough time.

The smile had fled from her face.

"You will start next moon."

"No," muttered Claude. "I don't want to."

"What do you mean, 'you don't want to'?" she snapped back. "Have you taken leave of all your senses? You think this is a matter of choice?"

"I have no desire to be an Acolyte." He held her gaze. Just. "I will not do what you ask."

A spark flashed from the Monvida's chest—blinding him for a second. He fought to open his eyes, vision turning heavy, hazy.

"I know your type! You do not like authority, Talador." Her tone was blade sharp. "Never have, never will. It is short-sighted. Very unwise." She hauled herself up, her bulk dominating the place. In one sweeping motion, she sent the table crashing to the floor. Paper scattered like startled birds, flying in all directions, and the totem skittered off towards the lift.

"Maybe." Claude's mind raced, searching for the right words. The faint green glow of his patches caught his eye, reflected in the totem's red. "I also wish to …" The words came from somewhere he could not explain, somewhere deep inside.

"Announce my resignation."

The Monvida's laughter erupted, bellowing around, rattling the frames. The sound grew louder as she came closer. The giant monkey loomed, almost within striking distance; heat radiated from her chest, hitting him like a furnace, matched by the fury in her golden eyes. She grabbed a fresh punnet of jaboticabas and squashed them in her palm, purple juice seeping through her fist, dripping onto the floor.

Claude hopped back a tad. "I don't mean this as an insult. I've enjoyed my time as an inspector. I could always—"

"Silence!" she boomed, breathing heavily, a waft of ferment. "What does your father do, Talador?"

"He's a treeper."

"Perfect." She picked at a muddie bite on her chin. "You will join those tailbrains in the trees."

"I guess telling work might be better suited to my skills."

"If you say so." The Monvida reached to the floor, picking up a cluster of the notes. They clung to her sticky fingers, enraging her further. With violent precision, she ripped the papers, the shreds flying from her hands, scattering like dead leaves, one after another. Peeling and flinging the stubborn remains over her shoulder.

"See those bits of paper, Talador." She let out an almighty belch. "That is what remains of your career."

"Understood," he said, tipping his head.

"Send Bain Longtail straight to me. Then go back to Hussleton, clear your cubicle. You begin your new job at dawn."

"As you command, Your Holiness."

"Oh, and give it back."

"Give what back?"

"Your badge, you silly, silly pichu. What a load of Monkey Business. Get out of my sight."

Claude placed the badge on the floor and bowed hastily. As he straightened, he caught movement in the doorway—a flash of wide eyes and small hands gripping the edge of the frame. She shrank back when her mother let out another belch, followed by a snarled wave of dismissal aimed at him.

He scarpered from the room, shocked the Monvida had not tried to grab him by the tail and swing him off the top of the TVA. As the lift doors slid shut, the last thing he saw was the face of Fuerza, grinning angrily at him.

***

Claude's heart raced like a hormiga late for work. He had no time to think. No time to waste. No time to realise the extent of what he had just done. The sheer stupidity of the timing. Drawing attention to himself. To the Refuge. *Now of all times.*

Something propelled his limbs forward without clear command. To the only place he could go. He rang the bell. Repeatedly.

"Who goes there?"

He recognised the voice. Dodge sounded suspicious.

"Claude Talador. I need to see Huckster. Is he here?"

"Of course he's here, he runs the place. State your business."

"I am here to see him. My business is blooming urgent."

"You're that State Inspector, aren't you?"

"Was," muttered Claude under his breath.

"Sorry, didn't catch that?"

"I am, yes, Dodge. *Now open the damn gate!* Or I'll have you fired for asking questions above your status."

Claude could almost hear Dodge thinking aloud in his tiny place of power. Then came a grunt.

"I'll open it." Followed by another pause. "Get in."

The familiar frame of Huckster awaited him inside. "My, my, my. What brings a State Inspector to these parts so early in the day?"

"We need to talk!" Claude gasped. "I'm not sure what I've done." Another breath. "I might have blown everything. I might have—"

"Woah, woah, slow down, my friend. Slow down. Let's take this up top."

Rain laced the air as they made their way through the Dump. It was a hive of activity already. The hideous scents greeted his nostrils once more.

Huckster bellowed, "Arabella! Can you come down a minute?"

The lookout's head poked out instantly. "Yes, sir, of course," she said, fluttering down rapidly.

"Mind if we use your nest for a bit?"

"No problem. Hello again, Mr Talador," she said, bowing low.

"Hey," said Claude, trying to muster a smile.

Things looked worse, not better, than they had been on Claude's official visit. The piles of waste were billowing over the edges of their enclosures. He ignored it for now, taking Huckster through the events that had brought him to his door.

"You're one brave pichu," concluded Huckster. "I'll give you that."

"Brave or stupid?" *I think I know the answer.*

"One can never know at the time."

Claude shook his head. "So how goes the plot for tomorrow?"

"As well as we could've hoped," Huckster whispered, even though there was no one else who could possibly hear them. "We take a backpack each. With enough provisions to last a moon cycle. Maybe two. From then on we must start to learn to live off the trees. Do as the Hundred did. We really can't know too much until we're beyond the mist. Not all of the party are natural climbers, we'll have to see. Maude has agreed to help us try to reach the abandoned crossing. Then she'll return with stealth to the Refuge. That gives us ten for this time tomorrow." Huckster stopped. Time seemed to get stuck in the mud before he spoke again. "Should I prepare one extra pack?"

"Well, I don't really have a choice now." Claude grinned.

"There's always a choice," said Huckster, a wry smile forming.

"No," said Claude. "I want in. I'm ready to follow you. To Maya."

"Brilliant!" Huckster pumped his fist. "But this is not a *follow* thing. We're all in it together …"

"I know," said Claude. *I don't exactly fancy navigating Shadowbor on my own.*

"Tomorrow," said Huckster, his eyes gleaming, "we should be out of this soggy mud pit for good."

Claude was not sure if he meant his Dump or the whole of Tierra Libre. Either way, a wave of excitement flew through his heart. It could not be contained.

Eyes Forward.

Chapter Nineteen

Que Le Vaya Bien

Luvé flows through us and everything in the rainforest. From the roots of the trees, to the granules of soil, to the moisture on the leaves, to the nerve endings of monkey knees. Do not seek to explain it. Or fully understand it. Only when you sense it, look to go with it. Do not obstruct it. Luvé is power. Energy.

- Adapted from Eliot Toussaint -

When the end-of-day whistle blew, Claude did not move. Usually, he would be the first to spring from his cubicle, making for the turnstiles before the echo faded. But today, he lingered, watching Beena pack up her things. He had thought of telling her, telling her everything. But what would he even say? *I'm leaving. Maybe forever? You coming?*

The words sounded absurd, even in his mind. Beena would not understand. Or worse, she would. The weight of responsibility. That was what kept her here, tethered to her work in Hussleton, confined within the bounds of Tierra Libre. It did not matter that she shared his dreams of escaping; her dreams ended where duty began. He could already hear her kind voice, shaded with resignation: *I can't leave, even if I wanted to, Claude. I have my family.*

But was that entirely true? Did she really want to stay? Or had the years dulled any glimmer of freedom? He had seen it in her before—so faint, yet unmistakeable—a flicker of discontent smothered by practicality. No. He knew it clearly. Not everyone could give themselves permission to dream. Not everyone could just up and leave. Beena's ties were strong. Stronger than her longing for something more. Even after what happened to Karo …

Beena glanced his way. "Thought you'd be halfway to your pod by now."

He forced a smile. "Just finishing."

She gave him a look, the kind that said she did not quite believe him. "See you tomorrow."

"Yep." He gazed at his desk. "Take it easy, Maitri."

Claude rummaged in his things, retrieving the pouch he had hidden—his salt savings, every gram and grain he had managed to set aside. It was not much. But enough to buy freedom from Floor 9, if she chose to use it.

Beena's cubicle was empty now, her chair pushed neatly under her desk. He slipped the pouch into her drawer, tucking it towards the back where it would not immediately catch the eye. On a scrap of bark scroll, he scrawled a single line: *Don't miss me too much.*

***

With time now of the essence, Claude sought solace, crawling his way down through the dirt, all the way through to its end.

He was pretty flustered. She was anything but. Carrying herself with a kind of grace and serenity so rare in Tierra Libre. Some greying fur around the temples and a glimmer of green added a certain mysticism to the keen eyes that delved right into a monkey.

"You mean to go," she said, without a hint of tension in her voice or posture.

She sees right through me, even before I speak. He took a breath. "I do."

"We could do with you here, you know." She busied herself preparing supplies for a row of backpacks. "A pichu of your disposition. Down the line, there could be the chance to really change things. That seems so far away right now, I know."

"I want to leave, Joan, that's all I know right now."

"And you must trust your own perspective," said Joan. "Do not worry, I will not beg that you stay, far from it. I only wish to say that a part of me will be sad to see you go."

"We'll make it to Maya, you know," said Claude.

"Ahh, the search for Maya," she said, voice soft and trailing. "I have heard those words before. The desire for freedom ..."

Her eyes were far away, lost in a memory or a different time.

She returned to him. "Maybe there is a wayward spirit in all of us. Or part of us at least."

"But you do believe such a place exists?"

"I like to believe in anything this State does not completely control. Whether that gives me the faith of a fool, I am not sure. One thing I know is that I will not be a monkey to dampen your dreams."

"We will find it." Although the borderbeings would take some interest in their arrival no doubt. He massaged his temples, easing the ache that had taken up permanent residence.

"I'm not sure Maya is a place to find in the way you imagine …" The corners of her mouth moved up. Almost imperceptibly. "Leave behind ideals, try to keep your tail gripped on what is real, and look for a place you want to call *home*."

Her cryptic ways puzzle me. And yet I value her way. She doesn't try to make my mind up. "Tierra Libre has never really felt like home for me."

"My grandmother said, 'Home is where your heart is'," Joan replied. "But if that heart yearns for somewhere different, then you could be on to something. Tom certainly seems to agree. There's eleven of you now, counting these packs."

"I believe so." He looked at her green. "Would you not make it twelve? Huckster said how valuable a mogician would be. And I would value you there—as a friend too."

She smiled, communicating without words. *What holds her back? What holds her here like Maitri?*

"Like I say, there is a wayward spirit in all of us, but, I must decline your invitation." She lifted a large pitcher and carefully poured into each water canteen. "I will go on with the Refugers that remain. Building and developing what we have here. It will take a long time. You cannot rush the holon process. But there will be more pichus like you, ready to open their eyes, needing that nudge along the way." She screwed the lid of one of the canteens. Tightly. "A monkey once told me it takes bravery to escape an environment you hate." She lined up the packs. "But it takes real guts to come back and try to change it. One moon, maybe we will hear songs in this rainforest again, feel proper sunlight on our fur, and the river will run a purer blue like in the stories of old. I will pray for your return, Claude."

She paused, her eyes glinting with a light that might have been a tear. "Have you ever been in love?"

Claude shook his head. "Not that I know of."

A faint smile touched her lips, as though she carried a secret he would not yet understand. "You will in time," she said, as if love were not a question of if but when. "Then you'll understand more of why I stay …" She pointed towards the door of the private chamber, the space where they had duelled so often those past moons. "It holds me, this place. Not with chains, but with roots." A pause, then, "Come now. Seeing as your heart is fixed, I have a few things for you."

An old wooden cabinet creaked open as Joan wiped the dust from its surface. The flickering light cast strange shadows on the walls, making it difficult for Claude to see inside. He squinted and crept forward. Joan reached in and took out an item. It was clear it was precious by the way she cradled it in her hands, turning it over, her expression thoughtful. *What in the name of Tiarra?*

Not what he expected. She passed him a wooden sword by the hilt. Not expected at all. Claude clutched it in his tail, twirling it round, testing the weight, seeing the detailed carvings etched on its sides. One side of the blade glinted brightly in the candlelight, firing a kaleidoscope of colours around them. A thing of beauty.

"This is yours?" Claude asked in awe, ready to pass it right back.

"No, never mine," she said. "I have simply been its custodian for a while. I took it on, knowing its power. Its legacy. Its destiny, you could even say."

"It's magnificent," he said, a strange sense he was meant to be here as a wave of calmness flowed from his head to his feet.

"Yetzara," Joan said, guiding him to test its feel. "That is its name. The two sides are opposite shades of the spectrum, light and dark. Both are needed in the world, within a soul. I hope it will be of practical value on your quest. Although I hope it will not be needed *too* much. You may notice its weight changes with your circumstances."

The sword's gleaming edge hinted at its ability to effortlessly slice through tangled foliage, sawgrass and any wild things that might dare cross his path.

"Thank you. Although I don't feel worthy of something so precious."

"Oh, I think you might find you are." She closed her eyes, waiting a moment. "And when you return, if you tell me of paradise, I shall tell you the story of this sword."

"Deal!" He grinned.

She took Yetzara from him, sheathing it and attaching it to one of the packs.

"Take this too." With a gentle movement, Joan extended her hand, delivering a small tubular vial into his awaiting palm.

It was about the length of a pichu thumb, a circular compass on the front and a simple stopper on its top. Inside, a strange translucent liquid morphed round in curious shapes. "There is powerful alchemy contained within, prepared by a mogician of greater esteem than me, from a garden of wonders. He insists it must only be taken at a time of great need." She closed his palm around it. "But, like I say, ideally, you'll have a peaceful climb."

"Another deal," he said, placing it in the backpack. *So many questions here. Yet, so little time.* "Why give me such gifts?"

She was not quick to answer. "Well, you said a mogician could be of value. And because I want you to succeed, of course. Find this paradise you monkeys dream of."

"I will certainly try," he said. "But why not give them to Tom?"

This time she was immediate in responding. "They are not for *any* pichu, Claude Talador. They are for you." Her shoulders tensed slightly as she counted the packs once more. Overly focused. *There's something else she's not telling me. Something important.*

"What is it, Joan?"

"I don't know," she started carefully. "Something troubles me about this plot. Something in my gut, hard to articulate. It has unsettled me." Joan shook her head. "Yet, I will not say don't go. The fear is for me to deal with, and I think it is fuelled by dark memories that cloud my faith."

Claude placed a hand on her shoulder.

"No, I won't thwart Tom's plan. The time has come." Her calmness was powerful. "The Blue Moon waxes, and it is not for me to stand in the way of forces beyond our control. You do have the green on you after all. Maybe it is inside you too.

"What do you speak of? You must tell me more before we go."

"Some things cannot be explained, Claude, only learnt. Certainly not in hours, possibly not in days, years even. You have Yetzara and the compass vial; these will help you. I only ask one thing in return."

"Whatever you'd ask."

"Even if everything seems to have changed from without, remember to still look within. To trust yourself."

He offered his tail. "Deal number three, Ms Saei. Although I feel I've got the better side of the bargain, I've offered you nothing."

"I do not think so. Just promise me this, Claude. When you go, do not just go to escape. Tierra Libre does not just need freedom. It needs renewal."

"Renewal?"

She nodded. "Yes. There is something special out there. Maybe not in Maya at all. I do not know what it is; perhaps no monkey does until they have found it. But I feel there is something. A seed, an idea, something we have lost here. Something essential. Luvé. Perhaps you will return with the most precious gift of all—a way to breathe life anew into this rainforest."

"I make that vow," he said, kneeling. "To return. To help you. And I look forward to learning the secret of the sword and all the other mysteries you hide!"

She lightened again at this. "You have strong blood flowing through those veins, that is for sure. May the light of Tiarra shine for you, Claude Talador. Que le vaya bien."

"Que le what?"

"You said no more questions, young monkey!" She chuckled. "Go now. Before I see sense and put a stop to this whole fanciful adventure."

He left her then, his movements faltering as he turned, watching as her mouth moved in a kind of silent prayer.

Her words lingered in his mind, and he sensed something profound. Something that held the power to shape his future. The path ahead remained veiled in mystery, waiting to be discovered. Claude could not shake off the thought that this moment would have great bearing in many moons to come. Short interludes with huge magnitudes.

Chapter Twenty

Once In A Blue Moon

*Tiarra had the ease and grace to befriend almost all. A light behind
her eyes that shone into others' hearts. Still, she knew when not to
trust another. She also knew that life is not a process to be controlled.
It could not really be tamed. Luvé released. That could mean a break
from the old. A new direction. A leap into the abyss of what is not
known.*

—From "Tome for Tiarra" by Viridia

The Blue Moon was already starting to glow iridescently
above ground. Below it, ten pichus gathered around the
table, eating slowly and in silence. The Refuge was eerily quiet, the
smell of incense strong. Claude had barely slept a wink the night
before and fidgeted through the whole day after. But tiredness
was not the feeling. He would be leaving Tierra Libre that night.
What he really felt was fear. Pure gut-wrenching fear that knotted
his stomach, clawed at his chest. The kind that would not simply
be shaken by thought.

Escape was the dream, but dreams were so much simpler

when confined to the realm of imagination. Now, on the edge of action, his mind became its own labyrinth of uncertainty.

What if I fail?

What if I'm caught?

What if the world beyond is no better than this one?

Yet, as his thoughts tormented him, they could not extinguish the flicker. Of something brighter. Hope.

A spark that refused to die. It whispered to him, urged him to believe.

How are the others feeling? Claude glanced round at his new companions. Trent Mallson, eager, practically vibrating. Maude, steady as ever, exuding determination. Dodge, the monkey from the Dump, was waiting beside a pichu who must have been his girlfriend. Tails linked, they seemed to be meditating. Ready for anything. Or at least trying to appear so.

Two younger treeper males he did not recognise hunched together, holding an air of stoic readiness. A pair of treeper females sat up beside them, chatting, faces alight. Claude smiled at their youthful energy, infectious spirit. Although their naivety no doubt shielded them from the dangers that lay ahead.

And then there was—

Musky! "Holy Mother of Fuerza," Claude muttered. *How did he get a spot on the team?* He doubted the professor would last more than a night outside their canopy. If they made it that far.

The eleventh member arrived at the table, looking weary yet fierce, scratching the polished fur beneath his chin.

"Welcome, my friends," said Tom Huckbane. "Welcome to the first evening of a new beginning."

Silent nods rippled around the group. Their new leader moved among them, tailoring his message for each monkey. He soothed their fears, kindling the fire of hope in their hearts.

He came to Claude. "Who'd have thought we'd be here with such a clear shot at freedom. A chance to leave this dark world, and right under *her* nose as well. A single leap and the poisonous waters will be behind us. A new life ahead."

Crossing the poisonous waters was a thought Claude preferred not to entertain. Instincts were better servants now. "Thank you, my friend," he said. "For leading us here. Helping me here."

"You found your own way here"—Huckster gripped him by the shoulder—"remember that. We'll go down in pichu history, that's for sure. Let's hope we live to tell the tales ourselves one day."

"I hope so too," said Claude. "And this may help us …"

He brandished the sword, Yetzara. Monkeys gasped Musky's loud intake of breath the loudest among them.

"The Verdan Emeral?" someone whispered. Almost too faint to hear.

Huckster masked his surprise with a low whistle. "Well, that's something!"

Claude passed him the blade. Huckster accepted it, curling his tail around the hilt. He hefted it once, testing its weight, then brought it up in a smooth arc. Two swift strokes swiped through the air. A smile broke across his face as he gave it back. "That will help."

Their leader made his way back to the head of the table. "Dare I say it, friends, the time is upon us. Gather your packs. It's time to head south."

***

The band of rebels travelled in single file through the moonlit rainforest, ears strained for any noises besides the deathwatch cicadas, chirping in their metronomic rhythm, accompanying the monkeys on their route through the trees. Claude settled to the rear of the troop, his pack digging into his shoulders, pressing heavily against his back. Sweat pooled beneath the straps, trickling in slow, irritating streams down his sides. He let his mind drift, falling into a detached headspace of motion.

Navigating the dense vegetation of Tierra Libre's deep south was no easy feat. Branches snagged at fur, thorny flora deliberately reached out to scratch beneath it. He heard the rain before he felt it. The droplets grew in size and intensity, transforming the ground into a treacherous quagmire that greedily clung to Claude's every movement, the mud latching on. Hidden traps lay in wait for the unsuspecting—or unfortunate—roots ready to trip, tangles waiting to ensnare, sinkholes eager to swallow the careless. Yet, a nervous excitement fizzed inside him, giving strength to his limbs. Urging him on.

After an hour or so, Maude called the group to a halt. Canteens were pulled out, and they sipped in the gloom.

Trent bobbed up beside Claude, eyes bright with excitement.

"Escaping! I mean, actually escaping! Are we really doing it, Claude? No more rules, no more leaders, no more office days. Can you imagine?" He did not pause for breath. "Do you think they'll write stories about us? Songs maybe? 'The Great Leap'—"

Claude nodded, pretended to listen. *Why can't the cicadas be just a little louder?*

Before long, Maude gave the signal to press on. Claude was relieved to have an excuse to move. He gripped the flaming torch with his tail, the flickering light casting elongated shadows. The weight of responsibility settled on his shoulders like his pack, but it steadied him rather than burdening him, instilling a strange sense of confidence. *We can do this.*

As they ventured deeper into the unknown, eyes scanned the ground, keen and alert. Every rustle of leaves or snap of a twig put their nerves on end. Claude's instincts had sharpened. Something about the place made him certain things could change at any moment. Gradually, the thick canopy began to thin, shadows fracturing and breaking apart as moonlight filtered through the foliage in dappled spotlights. It was like the forest was easing its grip, revealing a glimpse of what lay ahead—or a warning of what was to come.

Claude's ears twitched. *What's that sound?*

He raised a hand, signalling the group to halt. The noise became clearer. Recognition coursed through him. Tense shoulders loosened. The corners of his lips turned upwards. Murmurs of the Agumon River.

Raising the torch higher, he pointed it onward, motioning the group on.

The air grew cooler as they journeyed further south, medicating any notion of fatigue. The light lapping of water soon became unmistakeable. Maude, ever athletic and agile, took the flaming baton from Claude and led them at a brisk pace beneath the Blue Moon runway. Claude fell in behind her, growing anticipation matched by a growing unease. *Are we truly alone?*

Ears swivelling, he listened hard again. Nothing. Only the insects and breaths of his fellow monkeys.

Crunch!

His heart leapt before his instincts caught up. He withdrew his foot, eyeing the ground, then let out a sigh.

A snail.

He grinned at Trent, continuing on.

Reaching a vast forest clearing, the ten monkeys downed their packs with a collective exhale. The area was shrouded in an ethereal haze. A stillness. But no sign of Huckster. Claude took a large swill from his canteen and perched beside Maude.

Yet, the restlessness inside would not let him stay still.

Rising, he moved to the Agumon. It looked tame—calm, even—in comparison to how it appeared up north. Not the same beast, it did not rage down here. It did not foam or froth wildly. It was low, as they had predicted, although its dark waters still looked at least two pichulengths deep. Its calm surface concealed danger, deadly if one were to fall. The poison was reported to act within minutes. With no mercy.

A solid lump tried to form in his throat. His old fears of water becoming hard to suppress. Beside him, Trent babbled on. "The odds are actually quite favourable, Claude. It's simple, really. A leap, a swing, job done!"

I know, Claude could have said. *I know.*

But he also knew words were weak. Slippery, even when it came to the point of action. The chatter of the river toads this time provided ample cover from Trent's waffle. The youngster was saying something about why he had such faith in Huckster when it came—a new sound …

An alarming one.

A bloodcurdling howl.

No. Not here.

He had hoped he had left those creatures behind forever. That they would not venture this far south. But here they were. Not close. But not that far away either.

Unrest swept through the party. Nervous glances turned to frantic whispers and then to raised ripples of concern from all. An argument quickly ensued. Words colliding, drowning each other out. What was not drowned out was another call.

Louder.

Closer.

If there was anything more frightening than a howler, it was howlers on the move. Were they coming this way? Being deployed for something? *For us maybe?*

Claude's senses sharped, as precise as Yetzara's edge. "Stay calm." His voice sliced through the noise, not a plea, a command. The chatter fell silent. "Huckster will be here any moment."

"He'll need to be," said Trent, eyes wide. "We're sitting bugs here!"

"What if he's been caught en route?" Musky let out a squeal. "What if the Holy One got word of it? From one of us. From one we trust—"

"Don't be ridiculous!" Claude barked. "Get your packs, and let's head to the vine."

"He's right," said Maude, already slinging on hers. "Let's go."

Another howler call powered through the clearing, sending shivers down multiple spines. They wrestled with their packs, the sound of clicks. Claude fastened the buckle around Trent's midriff, fingers moving quickly where the younger monkey's had failed.

"We've been rumbled!" Musky spluttered. "Someone's betrayed us."

"Enough!" Claude growled.

Maude leant into Musky, whispered something to him, but the professor was beyond hearing, now hyperventilating, his breath coming in rapid gasps. Around him, the others fidgeted.

Claude's gaze snapped to Dodge and Candice.

Hand in hand, they moved quickly, steps a little jittery. They seemed desperate not to draw attention, but their haste made them impossible to ignore. "What are you doing?"

They stopped. Dodge looked back and shrugged. "I promised Candice we wouldn't hang around."

"We've waited our whole lives for this," she added.

"You can't just leave the group!" shouted Maude, eyes blazing.

"We have to," said Dodge. "See you on the other side, comrades."

The couple fled. Straight for the river and the black wall of mist.

Brilliant.

A rumble of thunder hit their ears, the rain intensified and darkness descended.

"This is the end!" screeched Musky. "We should never have done this. We're done for. Doomed!"

Trent slapped him hard across the chops. A large degree of spittle went flying into his face.

"Woah!" shouted Maude, jumping in to protect the professor.

Trent was not backing down. In seconds, he and Maude went at each other's throats, flailing limbs; the others shouted in garbled tones. Voices rose in a chorus of anger and fear; they pressed in together while Claude moved back.

A flash of lightning illuminated the clearing. For a heartbeat, everything stood still, bathed in stark, silver light. And that was when Claude saw it.

What the—?

Stood silently beneath the boughs of the surrounding palms, a masked monkey waited. They raised a hand, beckoned Claude over. The group, occupied with their squabbling, were unlikely to notice his departure. He set off towards the monkey, approaching warily. As he got closer, faint details emerged: speckles of grey fur and a tinge of red. Claude's tail shifted, poised at the hilt of his sword. The monkey shook its head and slowly lowered the mask.

It was you! You that gave hope from the shadows of the Refuge. "What are you doing here?"

"Evening, Inspector," said Ludere. "I've come to keep your Eyes Forward."

"And Huckster?" His absence made no sense. He had given them all his word. It was his plot.

"I am afraid he is not coming."

"What do you mean 'he is not coming'? I was with him earlier. He—" Claude's words tumbled out, laden with disbelief, mind racing to fill the void of explanation.

Ludere held Claude's gaze. "Tom cannot help any of you now. *She* has him. And she is coming for you."

Claude's brows furrowed. "The Monvida?"

"Yes, she is not too keen on pichus leaving her trees"— Ludere's tone was darker than Claude had ever heard, a stark contrast to the warmth that night at the Pen—"if she can do anything to stop it."

But Huckster had been their leader. To leave him behind—to take the leap without him—

"You must take them now."

"Me? You can lead us, Ludere. A monkey of your moons …"

"No," he said, shaking his head, a wry smile at the corner of his lips. "I do not need to escape to find what I desire. I will return to my garden and trust in Tiarra."

"What of Joan then? She must help now. Make the leap with us."

"Ms Saei is by the river." Ludere pointed in its direction. "Only her heart lies in this world, too, as you know. She will not cross. You must lead them, Claude. Find a way through the trees once on the other side. Make for the abandoned crossing with haste. Then maybe, after a great adventure, you will make it to Maya. Even come back to us in time. That is what I will ask from Tiarra." The older monkey gripped Claude firmly by the arm. "One bit of advice before you set off—follow the bird."

"What?" said Claude. "The one I've seen? How do you …"

"Try following it and touch wood"—he grabbed the nearest palm trunk—"you can be free." Ludere spun him round and put something in the clutch of his tail. "Take this. Now, go live your life!"

Claude obeyed, albeit with a multitude of questions dancing through his monkeymind. Ludere was right, though; there was no time. The howlers were coming. Fast.

One last bellow came from the old gardener. "Oh, and don't forget to have some fun on the way. La joie de vivre! It's your reality after all."

Is he for real? Claude returned to the troop with haste, the group turning towards him as one.

"Dodge and Candice had it true"—he addressed them all— "we must leave now."

"Huckster said to wait, d-didn't he?" said Musky.

"We can't wait here any longer. We'll end up dinner for the howlers." Claude paused and studied all the faces around him. None looked in uproar. None offered argument.

A loud howler call came in response.

How many do they have? They're closing in. Closing in on us.

"Those who have lost their faith, go now," Claude ordered. "East along the river. Take to the trees if you can; there you'll have a greater chance of safety. And you will have committed no crime. The rest of us—we make the leap. Now!"

The monkeys all looked at each other. The young treepers had clearly lost all faith and disappeared into the trees without explanation.

"And then there were four," said Trent grimly. He gave Musky a sideways glance. "And one with the wits of a hormiga."

"I have more wits than you'll ever have, Mallson," Musky snapped back.

"We may catch Dodge and Candice yet," said Maude with a hopeful look back towards the Agumon.

We'll need more than hope to survive this. "I doubt it," said Claude. "They look well suited for the challenge ahead." His gaze swept over the group. "Packs back on. Let's stay brave while we still can." *This would've been easier alone. Or just me and Maude.*

The quartet scrambled for their kit, Claude stowing Ludere's gift—*a nutcracker? Weird*—in the front pocket, and rushed to the riverbank. More ominous cries of the howlers echoed.

Trent bobbed on the spot. Grin wide and misplaced. "Alright, team! Time to catch this vine."

Claude shot him a look.

"Wait!" screeched Musky, clutching his pack like a lifeline. "Who first?"

"Me," said Claude, rolling his shoulders.

"And I'll be right on your tail," said Trent.

"Hold up. No," said Maude. "We must get Musky over first, and I will leap last."

"No! No, I can't go first—"

"You can, and you will." Claude buckled the trembling monkey's pack. "You'll be fine, Professor." He lined him up with the sleeper vine. The target was moving, almost imperceptibly. Backwards and forwards. Slowly. *Yes!*

A glance back to the Agumon; it looked a long way across. A long, long way. Straight into darkness. Claude's heart rattled against his ribcage now, attempting its own escape. Poor Musky was in a worse state, pulling the fur from his head, struggling for breath, moments away from breaking down entirely.

"Try to be calm. Trust the vine. One leap," Claude said encouragingly. "We were made for this."

"Made to be eaten by howlers?" replied Musky.

"What're you waiting for?" said Trent rather less encouragingly.

Without arguing, Musky started into an awkward move towards the target. Ungainly. His chances slim.

A pichulength from the edge, the professor halted. *Oh no!* Perching agonisingly forward, almost dropping headfirst into the river.

Maude acted fast and caught Musky by the waist, hauling him back from the edge. The pair tumbled over. A tangled mess of limbs and packs.

"Pull yourself together!" said Claude, helping them both up.

Trent had seemingly lost all patience. "I'm not waiting around!" The youngster made a dash for the river, reaching the edge, leaping with gusto.

Claude barely had time to react. "Trent—"

He soared through the air, arms outstretched. Hands reaching for the vine.

He's got a hold!

Trent careened out and away into the darkness. Released his grip. Going out of sight completely.

The clearing fell silent.

Tiarra, please!

Then, a muffled cry from the other side. "Woo hoo!"

He made it.

Claude looked at Maude. "You go now," she said.

The loudest howler call yet boomed towards them. And the rain fell harder, striking like tiny serrated pebbles. Shouts rose above the din.

Are we too late?

"What about him?" Claude pointed to Musky, spinning in frantic circles. A mess of a monkey.

Maude narrowed her eyes. "I'll hurl him over if I have to."

Claude nodded and turned to face the poisoned waters. His limbs shook a little as he tested the tightness of his own pack. This was it. A shot at freedom. A leap of faith ... *One I've waited for my entire life.*

He set off, resolve firm, dead straight at the vine.

Ready to jump.

Pwft!

A thud came from behind.A cry.

Claude swivelled. Maude stooped over.

No!

She flashed him a look of anguish, then sunk to her knees. A dart pierced her back, stuck right through. Its tip dripped black. Poison.

Thud! Another dart crashed into a tree beside them.

Whoosh! One missed Musky by a whisker.

The professor lost all composure and bolted for the trees. Much quicker than his arms and legs had moved for the failed leap.

Another cry rang out. In the distance, Musky's escape came to an abrupt end. Eager howlers rattling their harnesses. Their hormigas holding them back from eating the fool alive. The professor's arms, legs, and tail were put in binds. The hunting party turned to the two remaining Refugers on the bank.

Claude dropped to Maude's side. Snipped off the arrow tip with Yetzara and yanked out the protruding shaft. She grunted and balled a fist.

"Go," croaked Maude with a wistful expression. A thin layer of blood congealed around her chest, staining her fur; the paralysis was already kicking in, her head bobbing forward.

"I'm not leaving you behind."

"Go!" Firmer this time. A blaze of determination in her eyes. Resolve unyielding as her body weakened.

She would not accept further help, pushing him weakly in the chest. Back in the direction of the vine.

This is not what should have happened. She did not deserve this.

"Stop in the name of the Holy One!"

A poison dart whistled towards Claude's head. He ducked; it rushed right past him, shooting somewhere into the abyss.

"Hold your fire!" ordered Bain Longtail, his voice unnerving. "Remember the orders."

Claude turned, making out the group more clearly, reflected in a pale blue haze. Bain controlled a cohort of strong hormigas. Plus three howlers, baying for blood. *One would've done!*

A second pichu arrived. Right by the river on his left. Joan Saei. Silhouette clear. A touch of green. Tail raised high towards the moon. A small sphere of light brimming. Held between her palms. Startlingly yellow.

"Joan." Claude started to call out. But she moved.

With an arc of her tail, she brought the tip down, sending a bright spark streaking through the rain. Blasting out towards the pursuers.

Claude squinted, shielding his eyes against the intense light. Unsure what was happening.

"Saei, stop it at once," Bain called out. "This is Monkey Business of the highest order!"

The spark struck the ground, scattering the hunters and stealing their attention. Howlers snapped at the air. Joan gave a last beckon towards the river and then fled. Fast.

Claude pivoted back towards the Agumon. He was completely off line this time.

It cannot be!

A bird hovered, beckoning him on, the moon forming a spotlight on his course.

Claude padded furiously, eyes firmly forward. He jumped into the air, a vast void of darkness yearning to gobble him up. Heart thundering, he stretched out his hands, fingers straining, grasping for the vine.

Yes!

He clutched it with all his will. Using the skin on the end of his tail too. A firm grip. His stomach lurched as he swung out across the vast ravine. Soaring across the gaping chasm. Suspended over the yawning abyss.

The moment came.

He let go.

Air rushed into his face. He had propulsion, a fine leap.

Enough?

Sharp pain shot through him as he crashed into the opposite bank. The force knocking the air from his chest. Desperately, he clung on to a few overhanging roots, his breath coming in rasps. He had not fallen. With sheer determination, he pivoted back, levering his torso over the top, legs dangling precariously above the brown river. He scrambled upwards, ignoring the searing pain in his side. And the fear.

Furious shouts echoed across from the takeoff point. Angry voices, filled with frustration and hatred, carried through the mist. He refused to look back. Nothing for him there. Not now.

Scurrying forward on his four limbs, seeking any signs of allies, he pushed on. The mud slowing him, but not enough to stop him. No trace of Trent. No flicker of the bird. No trail from Dodge and Candice. *Nice of them to wait!*

He cursed the fortune of Maude. Musky too. But before the weight of despair could drag him under, a surge of something. A powerful force. One that came from his body.

Adrenaline.

Euphoria.

He was over the Agumon. Beyond the mist. Terra incognita.

No monkey had ever been outside Tierra Libre—so the history books told anyway. But here he was—Claude Talador. A free monkey.

And now officially an Enemy of the State.

To be continued …

Acknowledgements

The making of *The Monkey State* has been quite a journey, so the following has become quite a list. Inevitably I left it till the last stages to write (and edit). I am sorry for any omissions or inarticulate/insufficient gratitude.

Right, working in (rough) chronological order.

Family. You are the life-support machine.

Mah—thank you for the Claude proofreads at various stages, a financial injection for the craft, always providing a safe haven at Cricklade, our coffee chats, the writer/wanderlust gene and your reliable scouse humour.

J, for the unwavering love, so many special sibling moments and being a far better artist than me. You've married a top bloke in Rich and brought two top lads into the world too.

Dad, another better artist, who joked upon hearing a reader cried on finishing the whole series, "Is it that bad?" Cheers, mate! But no, you've always had my back and push me to be a better version of myself. A bit of tougher love is helpful when entering a world where not everyone will like you or your work.

The Creaby clan, I love you all. You've made Liverpool a second home for me.

A shoutout to the Mapsons. We've been through a lot and I feel lucky to have shared beautiful times with you all. Mappo, you've been an unbelievable best friend. Beck, you got me my first book writing book, *How Not to Write a Novel*. Pans, you've supported my writing journey from the very start. Thank you for everything. Pete & Em, you are great also!

Friends. The other half of the life-support machine. Fuelling me with laughter, questionable wisdom, sporting events, stag dos and unforgettable weddings. Even if you haven't been involved with the book, you've still been a great aid. No one writes in a vacuum and life very much goes on as you scribble. Miiker, Callum T, Clobs, Narsimh and Dan T, you deserve special mentions.

The amazing people I met travelling, your time will come in Book 2, and it'll make sense why if you make it that far with the reading.

Tim Ferriss, John P Morgan, MJ DeMarco, and, of course, Chris McCandless, for planting the seed that there might be another way than the corporate life. Not necessarily the right way but a way less climbed …

Escape the City were a key catalyst for the main theme of this story. A few there have inspired me particularly: Keeno, for his energy and limiting belief squashing; Skye, for her calmness and determination. Dom, for his vision, unerring work ethic and being an example of what a good boss can look like!

Jane C, for the early coaching and gateway to a different

kind of psychology. Michael Neill, George Pransky and the late Richard Carlson.

To Rich Jones, for being the first-ever reader and for doses of no-nonsense life advice along the way.

To Larry, for sharp developmental insights and comparison titles that have strengthened the depth of the monkey series.

To JMac, my wingman at the Palace, who took his time to read the beast that was Draft 3 and encouraged me to keep on going.

Pete B, for the steady supply of high-quality film stories that helped mould edits to the plot.

To Shawn and Tim at Story Grid, who in many ways I hate because they slowed down my process of getting this out … but have taught me so much about the writing craft through their books and courses—enabling me to run down my own dream.

To Wendy, my fellow pichu. You've been an absolute superstar from day one with jokes, pep talks, pick-me-ups, fur grooming and even mini interjections of project management. You've helped me so much practically (and psychologically) with the whole process. Living with someone who writes in their spare time can be a tough old gig. So I really appreciate your positivity about my work and patience with ever-extended deadlines while helping to keep the fun and flame of adventure going in our daily lives. You've also shown me that a compelling future can also involve another and is far better for it—2025 is our year.

To the Thorntons and Kennedys, thank you for welcoming me with open arms. Cora, I still have that pen ready to sign.

Mel, for designing the map from a limited brief and capturing exactly what I needed with professionalism.

To Jennifer, beta reader extraordinaire. Your comments were sage and timely. You also helped establish the book could work in chunks …

To Kathy, I like to think there is something greater at play that brought you into contact with me and the monkeys. I sense it's taken you on a journey too—trusting our Toucans. It's hard to put into words just how much you've contributed. Thank you a million and more. You've become an incredible friend along the way, and promise me you'll keep those Drunken Monkey Dreams alive … I heard this line in a Like Stories of Old video but taken from David Foster Wallace's *Infinite Jest*. I think it sums it up perfectly: "There may not be angels but there are people who may as well be." Although, can we have monkey angels?

For the agents that politely declined or ignored me, I thank thee for nudging me to self-publish, which ultimately is right for Claude. I'm happy to talk about film rights in the future though, aha.

Tom van der Linden, Paul Millerd, Dan Koe, Benjamin Hardy, Alan Watts and many others whose work or writing has inspired me in recent moons.

To Haz, David, James, Loren, Becky, Fern and the wider team at Swoop for showing me that adventure can also come while based on British soil, sculpting content and stories from my MacBook, helping facilitate other people's adventure stories. An enjoyable and rewarding form of work.

Louis, for the late injection of artistic solidarity. Mark for coming in at the final hour to rapid prototype a book cover and nail the brief in time for Christmas.

In slightly the wrong order now, and it's not possible to mention all the influences on the book, yet a special thanks goes to Crichton, Martin, Tolkien, Rothfuss and Rowling *et al.*, who create wonderful magical worlds for us to inhabit. Even if (for me) it is only in that half-hour window before falling asleep after a busy day. I hope the monkeys can help a few people dream in a similar way.

Lastly, thank you to you—the reader—for giving your precious time to these pages and characters. I am completely humbled that you've taken time to explore something I've put my heart, thought and hours into. I hope you've enjoyed turning the page. See you on the next book too?

About the Author

Jim has been dreaming up adventures since he first got lost in his dad's worn copy of *The Lord of the Rings*. These days he draws on his own experiences—escaping corporate law and travelling in the Amazon rainforest, Costa Rica and China (among other locations) to craft stories of his own.

Based in Bristol, England, he works full time as an adventure travel content manager for Swoop Patagonia and freelances as a feature writer for *Onscreen Magazine*. A former team member at Escape the City, he remains fascinated by debates surrounding the future of work.

When he's not writing, Jim can usually be found chasing a football, tinkering with his next creative project, or plunging into ice-cold waters.

The Monkey State is J. R. Roberts's first novel.

The story continues in …

Book 2 of *The Monkey State* Trilogy

In Search of Maya

Through the trees of the south and into the depths of
Shadowbor, Claude flees,
Chasing freedom, meaning and whispers of the fabled Maya
paradise.
In the shadows, Tia follows …
Her mission is clear: track down her own brother and return
him to the Monvida.
Unharmed.

Two lives.
Two realities.
Two differing perspectives.

And a journey where the only true map may lie within.

माया

Chapter One
Heard On The Hangvine

Siblings are a complicated species. You think you know them. Better than anyone even. Then they act in a way you can't comprehend. Sending your own worldview spinning. Demanding a decision. A question. Is blood thicker than water?

—From "Pichu: A Family History 6:9" by Perceval Musk

The summons had crackled through the treetops like a warning: *Report to the Monvida immediately.* No details, no explanation. It had been so faint it could have been mistaken for the distant hum of an insect swarm. But Tia Talador knew better. It was the pulse of a signal only an Acolyte would recognise. The call of her leader.

This could be her moment. Her chance.

Tia combed back her short fur, pressed her fingertips to her forehead as the familiar pressure built. Stress had a way of burrowing in. If you let it. But was that not part of the High Life?

She lowered her hand, exhaling slowly, glancing at the polished bark wall. A distortion of her reflection stared back. Her gaze snagged on the speckle of rushed coffee on her lips. A fleeting imperfection. She wiped it away with the edge of her thumb and turned back to her quarters—neat, private, entirely her own. She could not help but smile. The Dormor Trees—thin walls, no privacy—seemed like a lifetime ago. This, now—a just reward. But it was not enough.

Outside, the moon just about lingered on the horizon, its pale glow filtering through the canopy and fading into the edge of the sky. As rare as the Blue Moon was, Tia hardly spared it a thought. She had no time for the poetic musings of monkeys like her brother. The world did not run on stories or signs—it ran on power. And power came to those who earnt it.

The early hour suited her; time to think, to prepare, to be one move ahead. A certain victory in being up before the others—before the competition. Plus, the cooler air of pre-dawn Tierra Libre carried a sharpness she liked, a crisp promise of clarity before the heat of the day muddled everything. Life was good.

Tia closed her door with a soft click and descended to the canopy floor. The ground outside greeted her with a heavy squelch, mud clinging to her limbs, weighing her down. A reminder she was not made for speed these days. Not with her size. She wiped her hands on her thighs, a small concession to the grime, and adjusted her pace.

Sweat dampened the fur at her nape as she reached her destination and the air thickened under the canopy of heavy-set kapoks, their sprawling roots cradling the regal building nuzzled in amongst them. The path to its front door lined with freshly scattered bark. Scuffing it would leave an impression, a careless mark she did not want to make. She slowed; *no need to rush now I'm here.*

The rake-thin figure of Bain, their Head of Reality, emerged. His gaze swept over her with the precision of a monkey accustomed to measuring every detail. Every flaw. Every deviation.

"Good morning to you, Talador." He tipped his head.

"To you too, Longtail."

His eyes narrowed a touch. Just enough to remind her who held the advantage here. "You're a little early."

"I thought it best to—"

"You thought wisely." His interruption came with a flash of his perfect teeth, a quick look at the outside world, then back to Tia. "I will see if she is ready for you now."

Anxiety flickered. Still, Tia slowed her breathing and waited. Longtail vanished inside, leaving her alone in the quiet. The faint sound of a fountain reached her, seemingly coming from beyond the building. Her attention shifted to the two statues flanking the triangular porch entrance. Caiman heads grafted onto monkey bodies. Sura had told tales of the lizards before … dangerous, relentless, impossible to outrun. These ones at least were harmless. Just wood. She ran her tail along one. Cool to the touch. The carved faces seemed to hover between a sneer and a grin.

Creepy. She shivered, pulling her tail back. *The world is definitely better off without you.*

No guards? She glanced around again. *Strange.* This was the Monvida's sanctum. She had expected a greater security presence, a show of power befitting their leader.

The door creaked open. "Come in," said Bain.

Tia took another breath and moved forward, following him inside. The grand entrance hall greeted with the warm heady embrace of tropical plants. Towering stems and broad leaves crowded the place, their verdant greens broken by the majestic colours of orchids. As they went through to a kitchen, the wafting smells of wild herbs and spices forced her to lick her lips.

Bain continued to say nothing, leading her through a long corridor. Each closed door they passed hinted at secrets. Ahead, an archway framed an entrance to a well-manicured jungle garden. It sprawled endlessly, the size of two nutball pitches at least. In the centre, a striking tower-like palm tree created a wide pool of shade. Beneath its fronds sat the giant monkey— her leader—facing out into the wider rainforest. Basking in the relative tranquillity of her own pocket of paradise. Two hormigas hovered by her side, frantically fluttering banana leaf fans. They showed no sign of discomfort. No indication it was a chore. This was not servitude—it was devotion.

"Your Holiness," Bain said clearly. "She's here."

The Monvida turned around. Her eyes shadowed but sharp. She gestured for them to join her.

"You look tired, Talador," she said. "What can I get for you? Fresh coffee. A cold glass of ferment?"

Is this a trick? "What are you drinking, Holy One?"

"Coffee this morning. It is a day for a clear head."

"I'll do the same then."

The Monvida clicked at the hormigas, signalling for two fresh vessels to be poured. Not three. "Leave us be now, Longtail," she said. "Thank you."

"You are sure?" Bain asked.

She did not answer. Her silence more final than any word.

Of course she's sure.

Bain muttered something imperceptible and left as if carrying the weight of an unfinished conversation.

The Monvida did not seem concerned. "What do you make of my royal residence then, Talador?"

"It's a fine home. I've not seen finer." The vista was one an ordinary pichu could only dream of, let alone experience. Her focus landed on a circular swimming pool. And then drifted to an enormous hammock. It could hold a—

"This garden, and the palace itself, were built at the bequest of the Monvida XXV," the Monvida said. "But he contracted a nasty bout of librengue fever only months before completion. And thus, he never spent a single day here. The next Monvida, a fearless female from Fuerza's lineage, inherited the prize and many moons later, I became the custodian of this pretty little paradise."

There's nothing little about it. "I imagine you wish you could spend more time here?"

"Quite so, my dear. Quite so. But it is not without its challenges.

The muddies can get lively on an evening. And it is an awful lot of work for my staff to keep any of the plants from dying."

"I can imagine," said Tia, sipping the fresh coffee—rich, dark, and undeniably one of the finest roasts she had ever sampled.

The Monvida's gaze roamed the gardens in a way that suggested she was choosing her words. "I have news that may interest you, Talador."

"You do?"

The Monvida paused. A small orange butterfly with brown markings floated right past her face, dancing backwards and forwards between the pair. Tiny and graceful …

One of the hormigas swatted it with the blunt edge of its blade.

"You idiot!" The Monvida's scowl was immediate and cutting. "Do you know how rare those things are? Pick it up and give it here."

The hormiga obeyed, bringing it over. The servant received a forceful slap. They staggered but did not wince. Or cry out in pain. They did move back a little though. After a bow.

"Get out of my sight," said the Monvida with a shake of the head; she studied the tiny crushed creature in her hand. "We had days when such things were plentiful in the gardens. Now they are preciously few. What a waste, what a shame. You have seen a butterfly before?"

"Only at the old emporium … when I was much younger."

"Yes, excellent, those large blue mariposas. Splendid things, really. Shame they do not fly freely round these trees anymore.

Or that the emporium had to be closed to the public. There was a trespassing incident, a mindless prank, no doubt." She lowered the butterfly carefully and placed it on the table next to them, fingers brushing its lifeless wings.

A new hormiga arrived in replacement, nervous speckles already on its brow.

"So, where was I?" The Monvida leant forward, voice commanding attention.

"You had news, Holy One."

"Ah, yes." Her eyes flickered with intrigue. "Did you notice anything unusual last night? After you left our gathering?"

Tia sought memories of the previous evening. She had suspected a new Acolyte was to be announced but that had not been the case. Her leader had seemed a bit subdued, if anything. "No. Not that I'm aware of."

"It was the Blue Moon."

"I went straight to bed, so wasn't that interested, to be honest. I like to get an early—"

"You really have no idea?"

A flicker of self-doubt crept in. Had she missed something crucial? Was this some sort of test?

"There was quite the event last night," the Monvida announced. "Whilst most were sleeping, a group of misguided souls found their way out of their pods and southwards. A plot to escape had been hatched. And quite remarkably—a few of these souls—got away. Over the Agumon, would you believe."

Tia's jaw slumped. This could not be true. "How? How did they—"

The Monvida picked at an angry spot on her cheek. "I was hoping *you* might be able to shed some light on that."

"Me?" Tia blinked, struggling to process. "Why would I?"

"Because"—the Monvida's voice filled with gravity—"one of the pichus that made the leap—was your brother."

The Monvida held Tia's gaze in a vice-like grip, as if probing for a concession. A glow of red came from her chest. The air became clammy.

"This is the first time such a thing has happened under my leadership," she said. "And I want to know for a fact that you were not involved."

"I knew nothing!" croaked Tia, a pain shooting through her skull. "It makes no sense. How did they escape? What are you going to do?"

The Monvida wore her half-smile. "We, Talador. We are going to find a quick solution. Go with Longtail and gather all the Acolytes. At once."

Tia rose awkwardly, her face hot as a roaring fire. "Of course. I'll find him."

"Do not fret, my dear. Such is life sometimes, though these things happen." The Monvida's tone was soft now. Scarily so. "What matters is how we respond. With clarity."

"I'll sort this. I won't let him shame the Talador name."

"It may be too late for that."

***

She had expected grim faces—tight-lipped Acolytes with fretful expressions and whispers laced with unease. But something else filled the air at the top of the Treetop of Valiant Ascendance.

Excitement.

Seemingly there was nothing quite like the problem of monkeys escaping Tierra Libre to get the juices running.

"Morning all," said the Monvida, voice cutting through the low murmur. "Thank you for coming up here at such short notice. Listen carefully. We do not have much time."

The Monvida sat tall in her elevated chair, Bain at her right hand, giving nothing away. Tia glanced at the other Acolytes. The scene reminded her of school—all lined up and waiting for a lesson. Three hormigas flittered about their leader, offers of fresh ferment and nuts waved off with a flick of her tail. Her chest still flushed a faint red—a betrayal of irritation beneath practised control.

Stop staring.

Tia's mind snagged on Claude and refused to let go. *The idiot. What was he thinking? Did he even think at all? Probably not. That would be just like him—acting first, leaving everyone else to deal with the fallout.*

And now here she was, choking on the mess he had made.

"A proper search party will be assembled and sent out for our new Enemies of the State. Traitors to the Tribe."

Enemies. Traitors. The words dropped like stones. Claude was her brother. Reckless and infuriating and impossible, yes. But a traitor …?

"This will be kept as quiet as possible," the Monvida continued. "It goes without saying I do not want this carrying loudly on the jungle drums. We want their return secured—quickly and discreetly."

The emphasis on *discreetly* was not lost on Tia. But how could they keep something like this under wraps? The jungle already hummed with half-heard rumours, the gaps in the truth ready to be filled with exaggerations and lies.

The Monvida nodded to her favoured Acolyte. "Longtail, offer a précis on how we have got to this point."

Longtail did as he was told, talking through the evening events to all those gathered. Although, everyone here knew a version of the story already; the news had spread faster than dawn had appeared. But hearing it laid bare made the pit in Tia's stomach deepen.

"There is the one who evaded apprehension within our trees. Some fled early—driven by fear. And there are other pichus who know about this place they called the Refuge. Lurking in the shadows now, no doubt. They will all face the full wrath of the State."

The Refuge? Refuge from what? What kind of madness has Claude got himself tangled in this time? It sounds like something out of the old tales— idealistic and doomed.

"Yes, well put, Longtail," said the Monvida. "Now, one of you here this morning will be required to lead the hunting party on the ground." Her golden-eyed gaze seemed to probe all those present. "I would like to know if there is anyone up for the challenge?"

A challenge. That was one word for it. The heat of the Holy One's luvé brushed past Tia. Around her, Acolytes shifted, tails curling, hands twitching.

No one was forthcoming. The hesitation telling. Of course no one would volunteer—not for this. A mission outside the trees of Tierra Libre was not just dangerous, it was potentially deadly. The jungle beyond was not theirs anymore, if it ever had been. Who knew what really lurked out there? Would anyone even come back? Her mother had—

"Don't all jump at once!" the Monvida bawled.

She can't be surprised, can she? Tia's breath became a little short. Even if they found all the pichus—and quickly—it would surely not end well. Not for them, not for the hunters, and certainly not for Claude.

And yet …

Her tail rose before she could think better of it, holding it as still as she could manage. "Holy One, you could send me," she said, forcing her voice to stay steady. "I, of course, know one of them."

The Monvida pursed her lips.

Another tail shot up, its sharpness almost mocking Tia's careful resolve. "I would be better suited," said Serpa, an Acolyte to Tia's left. "And less … emotionally attached."

She did not turn to look. She did not need to. Serpa had been waiting for this opportunity ever since she joined. Always posturing, baying for power. Of course she would seize this moment, presenting herself as the logical choice—untainted by the mess of family vines.

The Monvida tilted her head, slowly, side to side, as if weighing things up in her mind. A whisper to Bain. Another pause, then a solemn nod. "Serpa will lead."

A sharp sting bit into Tia's lip as she willed her expression to remain neutral, but the heat rising in her cheeks betrayed her again. She had put herself forward, spoken up when no one else had dared. What more could she do?

And Serpa's smirk was practically audible.

"Talador," the Monvida said. "You will go too. Your inside knowledge—and intelligence—will be of value to this party."

Tia sprang to her feet, a spark of purpose "Yes, Your Holiness."

"Let's get this hunt going then," drawled Serpa. "I look forward to delivering the traitors back into your care." She addressed the Holy One but looked straight at Tia; Serpa had drawn back the bow, aimed and fired.

"This is no game of hide-and-seek," said the Monvida. "I want No Monkey Business, and they must not reach Shadowbor."

Her tail shot out and she grabbed Serpa by the forearm. "And I want Claude Talador returned to me unharmed. Is that understood?"

"Sure," murmured Serpa, recoiling slightly. "No Monkey